Kitty's Magic

Misty the Scared Kitten

Shadow the Lonely Cat

Ruby the Runaway Kitten

The Kitty's Magic series
Misty the Scared Kitten
Shadow the Lonely Cat
Ruby the Runaway Kitten
Star the Little Farm Cat

Coming soon
Frost and Snowdrop the Stray Kittens
Sooty the Birthday Cat

Kitty's magic

Misty the Scared Kitten

Shadow the Lonely Cat

Ruby the Runaway Kitten

Ella Moonheart

illustrated by Lindsay Dale and
Dave Williams

BLOOMSBURY
CHILDREN'S BOOKS
NEW YORK   LONDON   OXFORD   NEW DELHI   SYDNEY

BLOOMSBURY CHILDREN'S BOOKS
Bloomsbury Publishing Inc., part of Bloomsbury Publishing Plc
1385 Broadway, New York, NY 10018

BLOOMSBURY, BLOOMSBURY CHILDREN'S BOOKS, and the Diana logo
are trademarks of Bloomsbury Publishing Plc

Misty the Scared Kitten and *Shadow the Lonely Cat* first published in Great Britain in August 2016 by
Bloomsbury Publishing Plc
Published in the United States in February 2018 by Bloomsbury Children's Books
Ruby the Runaway Kitten first published in Great Britain in February 2017 by Bloomsbury Publishing Plc
Published in the United States of America in June 2018 by Bloomsbury Children's Books
Bind-up published in the United States of America in June 2018 by Bloomsbury Children's Books

Misty the Scared Kitten and *Shadow the Lonely Cat* text copyright © 2016 by Hothouse Fiction Ltd
Illustrations copyright © 2016 by Lindsay Dale
Ruby the Runaway Kitten text copyright © 2017 by Hothouse Fiction Ltd
Illustrations copyright © 2017 by Dave Williams

Bloomsbury books may be purchased for business or promotional use. For information on bulk purchases
please contact Macmillan Corporate and Premium Sales Department at
specialmarkets@macmillan.com

ISBN 978-1-5476-0114-1 (bind-up)

Library of Congress Catalog-in-Publishing Data
Misty the Scared Kitten LCCN: 2017021022
Shadow the Lonely Cat LCCN: 2017021037
Ruby the Runaway Kitten LCCN available upon request

Typeset by RefineCatch Limited, Bungay, Suffolk
Printed and bound in the U.S.A. by Berryville Graphics Inc., Berryville, Virginia
2 4 6 8 10 9 7 5 3 1

All papers used by Bloomsbury Publishing Plc are natural, recyclable products
made from wood grown in well-managed forests. The manufacturing processes
conform to the environmental regulations of the country of origin.

To find out more about our authors and books visit www.bloomsbury.com and sign up for our newsletters.

Kitty's magic

Misty the Scared Kitten

Chapter 1

"Grandma! Grandma!" shouted Kitty Kimura excitedly. "A postcard's arrived from Mom and Dad!"

Kitty ran to the kitchen. Emails were nice, but she loved getting real mail! The card had a picture of a waving ceramic cat on it. In Japan, it was a sign of good luck. Her parents were in Japan again now.

Grandma was pouring tea into her

flowery cup. She smiled as Kitty read the short message aloud and then stuck the postcard on the fridge.

Kitty's grandma was born in Japan, but moved to the United States when Kitty's dad was little. Kitty's parents now owned a shop that sold special Japanese things, and Kitty loved all the silky kimonos, colorful fans, and sparkly cell phone charms. Three times a year, her parents went to Tokyo to look for new things for the shop.

Grandma lived with Kitty and her parents, so they spent lots of time together, especially when Mom and Dad were away. Kitty missed them, but she loved being with Grandma. She and Grandma even looked alike, with the

same dark-colored eyes. But Kitty's hair
was long and black, while Grandma's
bob had a streak of pure white on one
side of her head.

"What shall we do for the rest of the
week, Kitty-cat?" Grandma said.

Kitty's real name was Koemi, but she

loved cats so much that she was given the nickname Kitty, and now everyone called her that!

Just as Kitty was about to answer, the phone rang.

"I'll get it," Kitty offered, running into the living room.

She picked up the phone. "Hello?"

"Kitty!" said an eager voice. "It's me, Jenny!"

Kitty was surprised. Jenny was her best friend, but they hardly ever called each other, because Jenny lived only three houses away. "Hi!" she replied.

"Can you come to my house for a sleep-over tonight?" Jenny burst out. "I have something really exciting to show you!"

Kitty giggled. Jenny was always

cheerful, but today she sounded even happier than usual. "What is it?" she asked.

Jenny paused for a second. "Well . . . I was going to keep it a surprise until you got here, but I can't wait. I've got a kitten!"

Kitty gasped. "Jenny, you're so lucky!" she said, a smile spreading over her face. "Why didn't you tell me before?"

"I didn't know until today!" Jenny explained. Kitty could hear her friend bouncing up and down excitedly. "Mom kept it a surprise until I got home from school. My aunt Megan is moving to England and she couldn't take her kitten with her—so she's given Misty to me! Wait till you see her, Kitty. She's gorgeous. She's pale gray with darker gray stripes. Mom says she's a silver tabby. And I think she likes me already. As soon as Aunt Megan brought her over, she ran straight up to me and rubbed herself all around my ankles!"

"I can't believe it," Kitty said wistfully. "I *love* cats."

"I know! That's why I called you right away," Jenny replied. "It'll be as if she's your cat too! So can you come? We can play with Misty all evening!"

"Let me ask Grandma," Kitty told her friend. "I'll call you right back!"

She put down the phone and raced back into the kitchen. "Grandma!" she called breathlessly. "Can I sleep over at Jenny's house tonight? She just got a *kitten*!"

Grandma put down her teacup. "A kitten?" she replied slowly. "Well, that's lovely for Jenny . . . but, Kitty, you know you start to sneeze as soon as you're anywhere near a cat."

Kitty bit her lip. It was true. Ever since she was a baby she had been allergic to cats. It made her feel sad and a little angry, because cats were her favorite animals in the whole world. She loved their bright eyes, their silky fur, and the soft rumble of their purring.

Most of all, she liked imagining what the cats in her village got up to at night, when people were fast asleep! What made it even harder was that cats seemed to really like *her*, too. They always followed her down the street, rubbing their soft heads against her ankles and meowing eagerly. Kitty couldn't resist bending down to stroke them, but she always ended up with sore eyes and a runny nose.

"Oh, please, Grandma," she begged. "I'll take lots of tissues, and if I start to get itchy eyes or a tickly nose, I'll stop playing with Misty right away, I promise."

Grandma gazed thoughtfully at Kitty. "Well, maybe you are old enough now," she murmured softly, with the hint of a smile on her lips.

"What do you mean, Grandma?" asked Kitty, frowning. *Old enough that my allergy will be gone?* she thought, confused.

"Never mind," Grandma told her, shaking her head. "Wait here, sweetheart. I have something for you."

Kitty bit her lip, curious. Grandma sometimes acted a bit strangely. She took long naps at funny times, and she would stay up late, saying she was watching her favorite TV programs. But now she was behaving even more oddly than normal.

When Grandma came back, she placed something carefully into Kitty's hands. It was a slim silver chain with a small charm hanging from it. At first Kitty thought there were Japanese symbols on it. But as she looked more closely, she saw it was a tiny picture of a cat.

"Wow," breathed Kitty, slipping the necklace over her head. "It's beautiful."

Grandma smiled and reached under her blue silk scarf to show Kitty a matching necklace. "I have one too," she explained. "They have been in our family for a long time. Yours belonged to your great grandmother. I've been keeping it safe until the right moment. It's very precious, and I know you will take good care of it. Make sure you wear it at Jenny's house. I think it will help with your allergies."

"You mean . . . I'm allowed to go?" cried Kitty. "Thank you, Grandma!"

Kitty flung her arms around Grandma, though she was puzzled about what she'd said about the necklace. How could a piece of jewelry stop her from sneezing? But she was too excited to ask questions. She was going for a sleepover at her best friend's house, and she was going to play with a sweet little kitten!

Chapter 2

Half an hour later, Kitty and Grandma set off for Jenny's house, swinging Kitty's overnight bag between them. As soon as Kitty pressed the doorbell, the door burst open. Jenny's freckled face was flushed pink with excitement. "I couldn't wait for you to get here!" she said with a grin. "Quick—come and meet Misty!"

Jenny led them into the kitchen, where Jenny's mom and little brother, Barney, were painting. Jenny's mom washed her hands and made a cup of tea for Grandma. Kitty looked around eagerly for Misty. "Where is she?"

"Over there, on the windowsill!" said Jenny.

Kitty gasped as she spotted the little cat. "Oh, she's *so cute!*" she cried.

Misty was curled cozily in a beam of warm sunshine. She was a soft gray color, with darker gray stripes all over her body, and long silver whiskers. Her eyes were a pretty blue. When she spotted the girls, she sat straight up, pricked her ears, and gave a happy mew.

"She loves this sunny spot," Jenny said, reaching out to pat Misty's head. "Come and stroke her. She likes being tickled right here, between her ears."

Grandma was watching out of the corner of her eye. Kitty touched Misty's soft, warm head gingerly, feeling excited butterflies fill her tummy. Misty closed her eyes and purred happily as Kitty stroked her all the way down to her long tail.

"She feels like silk," whispered Kitty.

"I know. I love her so much. I still can't believe she's mine!" said Jenny, scooping Misty gently into her arms for a cuddle.

Kitty sighed. "You're the luckiest girl in the world, Jenny. I wish I wasn't allergic to cats. Then maybe Mom and Dad would let me have one too!"

Jenny raised her eyebrows. "Oh gosh— I'd forgotten about that," she said. "Are you feeling all right at the moment?"

But before Kitty could answer, Jenny's mom came over. "You're allergic, Kitty?" she asked worriedly. "I didn't know that. Are you sure you'll be okay?"

Kitty nodded quickly. "It's just a little tickle in my nose sometimes, that's all. I feel completely fine!" she said. Although at that very moment, she felt a twitch and her eyes began to tingle. She *really* wanted to rub them, but she ignored it. If Jenny's mom knew how bad her allergies could get,

Kitty knew she'd say they shouldn't have the sleepover. Even worse, she might never be able to stay at Jenny's house again!

"What do you think, Mrs. Kimura?" asked Jenny's mom, turning to

Grandma. "I've promised Jenny that Misty can sleep in her bedroom, but I don't want Kitty to feel poorly in the night."

Kitty noticed Grandma glancing at the silver necklace. *Please don't change your mind now!* she thought desperately.

But to her relief, Grandma smiled. "I think Kitty will be just fine," she said.

"All right, then," said Jenny's mom. "No staying up late, though, girls. You know it's a special treat to have a sleep-over on a weeknight." She added with a smile, "I'll take both girls to school tomorrow, Mrs. Kimura."

Jenny and Kitty grinned at each other. Now they had the whole evening to play with Misty—and a little bit of tomorrow morning!

Grandma finished her cup of tea and thanked Jenny's mom. Kitty thought Grandma gave her an especially long, tight hug goodbye, but she wasn't sure why.

Once Grandma had left, Jenny said, "Let's go to my room. I can show you all the special toys we've bought for Misty!"

They dashed up the stairs with Misty still curled up in Jenny's arms. She let Misty jump down onto the floor, and the beautiful tabby rubbed her pink nose against Jenny's leg, then started padding around, sniffing things.

"She explores by smelling every-thing," Jenny explained. "Aunt Megan said a cat's sense of smell is ten times better than ours! And they can see in the dark and hear much better than people too."

She picked up a squishy ball of pink wool and gave it a shake. Misty paused for a moment, her ears twitching. Then she leaped playfully at the ball, swiping it with her paw and knocking it from Jenny's hand. It rolled along the carpet, the wool unfurling as Misty chased it gleefully. Jenny and Kitty giggled. "She's so cute!" Kitty said.

They played with Misty for the rest of the evening. Even when Jenny's mom called them for dinner, Misty followed the girls downstairs and padded around their feet as they ate, looking

up at them hopefully. Afterward, they chose a movie to watch in the living room. When they settled on the sofa, Misty hopped gracefully onto Kitty's lap, gave a friendly meow and curled up in a fluffy ball.

"She really likes you!" Jenny told Kitty.

Kitty beamed and stroked Misty's velvety ears. She felt really lucky that Jenny was so nice about sharing Misty. And she felt even luckier that she had a new cat-friend! The only problem was her allergies. She tried not to think about the strange itchiness in her nose and eyes, but the more time she spent with Misty, the worse it got. By the time the movie finished, it was almost like her whole *body* felt odd!

Before she scrambled into her sleeping bag on Jenny's bedroom floor, Kitty pulled a packet of tissues out of her overnight bag and tucked them under her pillow. She hoped she wouldn't sneeze too much during the night.

Jenny dived into bed and Misty jumped onto the bedcovers to snuggle up by her feet.

"Sleep tight, girls!" called Jenny's mom, switching off the light.

"Goodnight, Kitty!" Jenny whispered happily. "Today has been the best day ever!"

"I know! 'Night 'night," Kitty whispered back. Before long, she was drifting into sleep.

Kitty's eyes flew open. It was very quiet in Jenny's bedroom. Moonlight was shining through a gap in the curtains. She knew right away what had woken her up: her nose was tickling like crazy!

She rubbed it, but it didn't help. In fact, that only made it worse—now her cheeks were itching and her ears were tingling. Suddenly, Kitty noticed the tickly feeling was spreading. The tips of her fingers and toes felt like they were full of fizzy bubbles, and there was a strange prickling all over her arms and legs. Finally, she began to sneeze. "Achoo! Achoo! *Aaaaachoo!*"

The bubbly, tickly feeling spread right through her, and it felt like her whole body was sparkling and glowing. Kitty gave one more enormous sneeze. "AAAAAAAACHOOOOO!"

When she opened her eyes again,

everything felt different. Her nose had stopped itching and her eyes weren't sore anymore—but something was strange about them. *I must have gotten used to the darkness*, she thought. *I can see everything much more clearly!*

Then Kitty thought something else was odd. Jenny's bed was much bigger and farther away. *How is that possible?* Kitty wondered. She looked around, and as her gaze drifted down, she stared in amazement. Where her hands had been before, there were now two small, furry black paws.

Cat paws.

Kitty cried out in shock—but the sound that came out wasn't a cry. It was a meow.

Kitty's eyes widened as she realized what must have happened.

I don't know how, she thought, *but I think I've turned into a cat!*

Chapter 3

Kitty gazed down at her paws. She couldn't believe they belonged to her! Carefully, she lifted one up for a closer look. It was covered in soft black fur, with a white tip like a little sock. Underneath the paw were five tiny pink pads. *Is that really* my *paw?* she thought. *But how?*

Then Kitty had another thought.

Jenny. Was her friend awake? Glancing up at the bed, she saw that Jenny was still fast asleep. But next to Jenny's feet, Misty was sitting up and staring right at Kitty, her ears pricked up curiously. Quietly, she jumped down so that they were facing each other, nose to nose. This close, Kitty could see each beautiful fleck of gold in the tabby's blue eyes, even in the darkness.

Kitty heard her own name, whispered in a soft, friendly meow. "Kitty? Is that you?"

Kitty gasped. She could understand her! "M-Misty? I've turned into a cat!" she stammered. To her surprise, the words came out in a meow as well.

"How did you just change like that?" Misty asked.

"I don't know," Kitty replied. "One minute I'm sneezing, and the next I'm a cat!" Maybe she was dreaming!

"This is so exciting!" said Misty, her eyes bright.

Just then, Jenny yawned and turned over in bed. Both cats froze.

"Maybe we should go somewhere else to talk?" Kitty whispered.

"Follow me," Misty replied.

She padded quickly out of Jenny's bedroom. Kitty hesitated, then followed Misty onto the dark landing and down the stairs. She took slow, careful steps at first, worried she might take a tumble. It felt so strange to be walking on four

unfamiliar paws instead of two feet—and to feel her new tail swishing along behind her!

In the kitchen, Misty trotted up to the cat flap that Jenny's stepdad had fixed in place that afternoon. She nimbly dived through it, landing on the other side with an excited little wriggle. The flap swung shut again, and Kitty poked her nose against it cautiously. She didn't want to get stuck halfway! She pushed it with her paw, then took a deep breath and jumped. She managed to get through in one try, but lost her balance as she landed, and sprawled on the grass.

"Sorry, Kitty," Misty giggled. "I should have held it open. This must be so strange for you."

"That's okay," said Kitty, pulling herself back to all fours and looking around excitedly.

Jenny's back garden seemed like a different world: a moonlit jungle, full of exciting sounds, smells, and places to explore. Kitty's cat eyes could see every blade of grass perfectly, and her sensitive ears could hear a mosquito buzzing at the other end of the garden! Looking around, she padded over to a puddle on the ground, shimmering in the moonlight like a mirror. She peered down at her reflection.

Instead of a small girl with dark hair, a little black cat stared back at her! Kitty gazed at her furry ears and the sprinkling of white whiskers on either side of her little black nose. All four of her paws were white and, as she curled her tail up into the air, she saw that it had a white tip too.

And what was that around her neck? Kitty looked closer. It was the special necklace that Grandma had given her—but it had transformed into a collar! One thing was different, though: the picture of the cat had disappeared from the charm, and now there was the outline of a girl instead.

"This is all so weird," Kitty said. "I don't know what's happening to me!"

Behind her, Misty meowed in agreement. "I've never heard of a girl turning into a cat before!" she said. "But I know who we can ask: the Cat Council."

"What's that?" asked Kitty. *This dream is getting stranger by the moment!* she thought. *But I guess I'm just going to have to go with it until I wake up—or turn back into a girl!*

"There's a Cat Council in every town.

It's where all the local cats meet to talk and help each other with problems," explained Misty. "I can't wait to go to my first meeting here. The Council and their Guardian will help you. And apparently this Council's Guardian is really special!" Her eyes were bright with excitement.

"What's a Guardian?" said Kitty. It sounded very impressive.

"Every Cat Council has an extra-wise cat who can help with any really serious cat problems," Misty told her. "I'm sure the Guardian will be able to help you, Kitty. Why don't we call a meeting for tomorrow night? It's done the same way everywhere, so all cats know what to do."

"Okay! So how do we do it?" asked Kitty.

"Watch!" said Misty. She padded up to the garden fence and scratched three claw marks on it, making a triangle shape, and rubbed her fur against the marking. She then made a long meow that echoed into the night. Kitty's ears pricked up excitedly as she heard other cats meow back in the distance.

"That's the sign that a cat needs help from the Cat Council," explained Misty. "If cats hear the signal, they check fences and lampposts for this special symbol! They'll be able to tell from the scent of my fur that I called the meeting."

Kitty gave the post a sniff. To her

surprise, she could make out Misty's unique scent.

"Wow," she said. She had so many questions for the Cat Council already, even if she *was* dreaming all this! "So cats can talk to each other?"

"Of course! Just like we are now. And cats can understand humans too," Misty explained. "So I could listen to you and Jenny chatting today." Her blue eyes lit up. "Jenny's great," she purred happily. "I'm so happy I get to play with her all the time! And I'm glad we're friends too, Kitty. It's going to be really fun having a human friend who can turn into a cat!"

Before Kitty knew what was happening, Misty gave a mischievous

meow—and then pounced! Kitty
squealed in surprise as she tumbled to
the ground. As she and Misty rolled
playfully in the grass, Kitty felt a
warm, happy feeling in her tummy

and then heard a low rumbling sound. She realized the sound was coming from *her*. "I'm purring!" she gasped.

This was amazing! Kitty decided not to worry too much about whether this was a dream or not. She was just going to enjoy it while it lasted!

But unexpectedly, there was a soft *thump* and a low hissing sound behind them. Kitty and Misty spun around, and Kitty felt her ears prick up and her fur stand on end. In the shadow of the garden fence stood a large Persian cat with fluffy white fur, glaring at them through mean yellow eyes. Crouched on the fence was a second white Persian, with an expression just as nasty as the first. With another *thump,* he bounded down into the garden.

"You are on *our* territory," hissed the first cat, flicking his tail.

"I'm Claws, and that's my twin brother, Fang. And guess what? This garden belongs to us," said the other cat, baring his sharp teeth.

Kitty gulped. The garden felt very dark and dangerous all of a sudden, and these cats were big. Misty took a brave step forward and gave her friendliest meow. "I'm Misty, and this is Kitty," she explained. "It's nice to meet you. I just moved here today, so—"

Fang interrupted her rudely. "We don't care who you are, New Cat," he spat. "All the yards around here belong to us now, including this one. So you'd better scram! And if we see a *whisker* of you here again, you'll be dog food!"

"B-but this is where I live!" Misty protested, her eyes wide in alarm.

"We don't care!"

The Persian cats stepped closer, their eyes narrowed into cruel slits, and began prowling in a circle around Kitty and Misty, who huddled close together. Kitty felt her heart beating fast and noticed her back was starting to rise into an arch, the way she'd seen cats do when they were scared. "What shall we do, Misty?" she whispered.

"Quick!" meowed Misty. "Run!"

She darted across the garden. Kitty didn't stop to think—she sprang past

the Persian cats and raced after Misty as fast as her new paws would carry her, just as the first cat swiped his sharp claws right where her head had been! There were angry snarls behind her, and Kitty glanced back to see Claws and Fang chasing after them. Quickly, she and Misty squeezed inside the thick hedge at the end of the garden. Misty backed away, but Kitty peered out of the leaves, panting hard. To her relief, the Persian cats stopped outside the hedge. Kitty heard them growling menacingly.

"You'll have to come out of there sometime," she heard Fang snarl. "And when you do, we're going to get you!"

Kitty turned to Misty. "Shall we make a run for it?" she whispered.

"I'm not sure," said Misty, looking very worried. "We might be able to sneak out and run back to the cat flap before they notice—oh—what's that?"

She nodded at the ground by Kitty's front paws. Kitty looked down and saw something glinting in the moonlight. Her collar! It must have fallen off as she squeezed into the hedge.

Turning it over with her paws, she saw that some tiny words were etched on the back of the silver charm. Without even thinking, Kitty read them aloud.

"Kitten paws to human toes,

Kitten whiskers, human nose."

Right at that moment, Claws lost his temper. "Fine—I'm coming to get you!" he growled, and Kitty saw him crouching down as he got ready to pounce.

Suddenly, Kitty's nose began to tickle. Her tail itched and her paws twitched—and just as the Persian sprang into the hedge, everything around her went dark.

Chapter 4

"Girls! Time to get up!" called Jenny's mom.

Slowly, Kitty opened her eyes. The sun was streaming through the gap in her friend's bedroom curtains. Jenny was still cuddled up in bed with Misty curled by her feet, and Kitty was safely in her sleeping bag. She reached for her necklace and saw that it was the tiny cat charm again—not a collar.

Kitty lay there for a moment as the memories from last night flashed through her mind. She remembered the amazement she had felt as she looked down at her furry black paws . . . being able to speak to Misty . . . the nasty Persian cats in the garden . . . and then, as she'd read the strange words on her collar, turning back into a girl. The Persians had been so shocked they had fled the garden as quickly as their paws could carry them. When she was sure they'd gone, Kitty had carried a trembling Misty back inside the house.

It had all *felt* so real, but . . .

Kitty sat up and reached over to

stroke Misty. "Can you understand me?" she whispered softly. But Misty just rubbed her head against Kitty's hand, purring.

Kitty felt a little bit relieved—and a little bit disappointed too. *It must have been a dream,* she told herself. *But it was the strangest, most magical dream I've ever had.*

Just then, Jenny stirred. "Kitty," she said sleepily. "Were you talking to Misty?"

Kitty felt herself blush. "I was only saying *good morning*," she told her friend. "Come on, let's get ready for school."

By the time Grandma picked them up from school that afternoon, Kitty had almost forgotten about her funny dream.

"How was the sleepover, Kitty-cat?" asked Grandma, bending down to kiss her hello.

Kitty thought Grandma seemed nervous. *She must have been worried about my allergies*, Kitty decided. "It was fun, Grandma!" she reassured her. "And I didn't sneeze much."

Grandma nodded. "That's good," she

said. "Is there anything else you want tell me?"

Kitty looked at Grandma, puzzled. "Like what?" she asked.

"Oh, nothing," said Grandma, shaking her head. "Come along, girls."

All the way home, they talked about Misty. "Why don't you come in and play with her again for a bit, Kitty?" Jenny suggested as they walked down their street.

"Can I, Grandma?" asked Kitty hopefully.

"As long as it's all right with Jenny's mom," agreed Grandma. "And as long as you're home for dinner!"

Once Jenny had checked it was okay, Jenny and Kitty raced through the house, calling for Misty. "I bet she's in that sunny spot by the kitchen window!" said Jenny—but Misty wasn't there.

"Maybe she's in the garden," suggested Kitty. They went outside and looked around, peering under bushes and behind trees. Kitty got a funny feeling in her tummy as she looked under the hedge at the end of the garden. Even though she knew she had only dreamed about hiding inside it last night, it still *felt* real.

"Mom, we can't find Misty anywhere!" said Jenny, as her mom came outside with two glasses of juice for them.

"Oh, I think she's in your bedroom," her mom replied. "It's odd. She was settling in so well yesterday. She seemed to love the garden—she kept jumping through the cat flap with a funny little wriggle, as if she couldn't wait to get outside!"

Kitty almost dropped her glass of juice in surprise. *Misty did that in my dream!* she thought.

"But today, she hasn't been in the garden once," Jenny's mom went on. "She's jumped at every loud noise and hidden under the sofa. When I tried to encourage her to go outside, she bolted upstairs."

Jenny looked worried. "I hope nothing's happened to frighten her. Let's go and find her, Kitty."

As the girls ran upstairs, Kitty's heart was beating fast. *Was Misty afraid to go outside because of the Persian cats? Had it been real?* She needed to talk to Misty—alone!

The silver tabby was huddled on Jenny's bed and gave a little meow when Jenny and Kitty knelt down to stroke her.

"Let's try the ball of wool again!" said Jenny, rolling it across the floor—but Misty didn't seem to feel like playing today.

"Don't worry," Kitty reassured Jenny. "She's probably just tired. She had a busy day yesterday, meeting her new family!"

Jenny nodded, but Kitty could tell she was upset about Misty. "Let's read your new *Animal Girl* magazine," Kitty suggested, eager to take Jenny's mind off it.

They read the magazine together and
were just filling in the puzzle section
when Jenny's mom called up, "Can you
come down and set the table, Jenny?"

"I'll be back in a minute," Jenny told Kitty. Kitty nodded, her heart pounding. This was her chance! The moment she heard Jenny's footsteps thumping downstairs, Kitty turned to Misty and looked right into the tabby's blue eyes.

"Misty," she said quietly, "maybe I'm just imagining things . . . but was last night real? Did I turn into a cat?"

She waited for a second and felt her cheeks flush. She was going to feel so silly if this was all in her head! But to her amazement, Misty reached out a paw, placed it gently on Kitty's hand, and meowed emphatically.

"I *knew* it felt real!" gasped Kitty. "And is the reason you haven't been

outside all day because of those horrible cats, Fang and Claws?"

Misty gave a frightened little shiver. Kitty stroked her head comfortingly—

and then remembered something else. "The Cat Council!" she breathed. "You called a meeting with them for tonight. We can ask them what to do about those cats—and find out why I can turn into one!"

Misty's little ears twitched and she glanced towards the door. Kitty listened and heard Jenny coming back upstairs. "Meet me in my backyard tonight!" she whispered quickly. "I live three houses away—it's the one with the oak tree and the playhouse." Misty tilted her head to one side, looking worried. Kitty stroked her reassuringly. "It will be okay, Misty. Just make sure those nasty cats aren't around, then make a run for it." The little cat looked up at Kitty and meowed quickly in agreement.

As Jenny came back into the room, Kitty turned back to the word search they had been doing—but she could barely concentrate. Her whole body was tingling. What was going to happen tonight?

Chapter 5

Kitty was desperate for bedtime that evening. As soon as she and Grandma had eaten dinner, she raced upstairs and put her pajamas on. Grandma chuckled when she saw them. "Are you tired, sweetheart?" she asked, her eyes twinkling. "Your sleepover must have worn you out!"

Kitty smiled. Sleeping was the last thing she was going to do!

Grandma read a story with Kitty, then pulled the curtains closed. "Goodnight," she said softly and shut the door. Kitty listened to Grandma pottering around in the kitchen before eventually going into her own bedroom. Finally, the house was quiet.

Kitty threw back the covers, tiptoed downstairs, slipped outside, and stood barefoot on the moonlit grass. She squinted, wishing her human eyes could see as well as her cat eyes. But even in the darkness, she could tell that Misty wasn't there. *She must have decided she's too frightened of Fang and Claws to come*, Kitty thought, feeling disappointed. *How will I find the Cat Council now?*

Then she heard a meow from above her head. She looked up and saw a little cat perched in the oak tree. "Misty!" she whispered happily. The silver tabby leaped down and landed lightly on the grass, rubbing her furry head around Kitty's ankles.

"Now I just need to turn into a cat!" whispered Kitty. She tried to remember exactly how it had happened last night. Her nose had been itching, and she'd sneezed . . .

"I'm going to need your help!" Kitty told Misty. She bent down close and buried her nose in the tabby's silky fur. Right away she could feel the itchy feeling in her nose, and a noisy sneeze burst out of her. "Aaaaaaa CHOOOO!"

Kitty crossed her fingers for luck and waited. She could feel the sparkling,

shimmering sensation spreading through her body again. She gave one more big sneeze—"AAAAACHOOOO!"—and when she opened her eyes, she was whisker to whisker with Misty.

"It worked!" purred Misty.

Kitty looked around the yard. She could see more clearly, and every sound was sharper, from the rumble of Misty's purr to the *chirp-chirp* of a grasshopper on a nearby branch. Kitty swished her tail, twitched her whiskers, and practiced trotting around on her padded paws, getting used to being back in her cat form. "Thanks, Misty!" she meowed. "I'm so glad you're here. I thought you weren't coming!"

"I was nervous about those horrid

Persians," Misty admitted. "I heard them prowling around. That's why I hid in the tree until you came outside!"

"We can't let them bully you, Misty," Kitty told her friend firmly. "You've been stuck inside all day because of those mean cats! Let's hope the Cat Council can help."

"And tell us why you're turning into a cat too!" added Misty. "Come on, let's go. I've never been to this Council's meeting place before, but we can use our noses to find the way."

Kitty stared. "Really?"

Misty raised her head and sniffed. Then she padded over to Kitty's playhouse, jumped onto the roof, and from there leaped onto the back fence. "This way!"

Kitty followed cautiously. She wasn't sure she'd be able to jump onto the playhouse roof—it seemed very high!

"Crouch low on all four legs," Misty called encouragingly. "Then spring up! It's easy."

Kitty crouched, took a deep breath, then pushed off. She didn't jump quite high enough and had to scrabble with her paws to get onto the roof—but she'd made it! Jumping onto the fence was easier. "My legs feel so strong!" she meowed, gazing around. "And we're so high up. I can see into every yard on the street!"

"Now, use your claws to grip the fence and your tail for balance," Misty explained, sniffing again to check they were going in the right direction.

"Slow down—I might fall!" said Kitty, carefully putting one paw in front of the other. But to her surprise, she could trot along just as quickly as Misty, her tail swaying from side to side. She followed Misty along the fence, onto a shed roof, and down an alleyway. They emerged in a patch of woodland that was full of bluebells.

"This must be it!" whispered Misty excitedly.

Kitty saw a group of cats sitting in a circle. As Kitty and Misty padded up to them, they turned to look at the newcomers. Kitty swallowed nervously. They had arrived at the Cat Council!

As Kitty and Misty got closer, some of the cats stepped aside to let them walk into the middle of the circle. *I've never seen so many cats together before!* Kitty thought. There were silver tabbies like Misty, sleek gingers, tortoiseshells, fluffy grays with big blue eyes, and even three kittens with fur the color of honey.

The biggest cat was a tabby tom, who meowed sharply to get everyone's attention. *He must be the Guardian*, Kitty guessed. Then she noticed a small, dainty black cat with a white patch by her ear, her tail curled neatly around her paws. She was sitting quietly, but Kitty had a feeling she was important. Before Kitty could find out, the tabby tom made an announcement in a deep, serious voice.

"As our new members have arrived, it's time to open our meeting by saying the Meow Vow," he said.

Kitty listened in wonder as the cats recited what sounded like a poem.

"When you meow,
We promise now,
This solemn vow,
To help somehow!"

Once the Vow was finished, the tabby padded forward. "My name is Tiger," he meowed importantly. "My human is Mr. Thomas, on Beech Lane."

Kitty's eyes went wide. "That's my teacher!" she whispered to Misty. "I didn't know he had a cat."

A plump, fluffy gray stepped up next. "I'm Smoky," she said in a friendly meow. "I love naps, sleeping, and snoozing. It's nice to meet you."

Another jet-black cat stepped forward. His green eyes were friendly, but

he seemed shy. Kitty thought she'd seen him up on the hill in town, near her school. "My name's Shadow," he meowed, and Kitty replied with a friendly meow of her own.

As the cats introduced themselves, Kitty found herself purring happily along-side Misty. Now only the small black cat with the white patch was left. Kitty noticed the cat was wearing a collar that looked exactly like her own. "Misty, look!" she whispered. But before she could say anything else, Tiger spoke again.

"Welcome to you both," he began. "I understand, from the scent message we found earlier today, that you called this Cat Council?" He nodded at Misty. "Please tell us how we can help."

"Yes. My name is Misty, and I have a problem," she explained. "I love my new human, Jenny. But last night, I met two nasty cats in my garden. They chased me and my friend Kitty and said they'd turn us into dog food!"

The gathered cats hissed at Misty's story, their whiskers shaking. "Did they have fluffy white fur?" a silky Siamese named Biscuits asked nervously.

"Yes!" replied Misty. "Do you know them?"

"I'm afraid we do!" sighed Tiger. "We've had problems with Fang and Claws for months. We've tried to give them a stern talking-to, but they just ignore us, and after a while they're back at their old tricks!"

"Not long ago, they sneaked through my cat flap and ate all my special treats," explained Biscuits sadly. "They made a huge mess in the kitchen. My human got very cross and shouted at me!"

"They jumped into our yard when we were playing," added one of the tiny honey-colored kittens. "We were so frightened that we hid in the shed!"

Tiger exchanged a glance with the small black cat with the white patch. "Enough is enough. We're going to do everything we can to make sure that Fang and Claws stop this once and for all!"

Misty purred gratefully, then turned to Kitty. "My friend has something she needs to ask about too," Misty said,

nudging Kitty with her nose encouragingly.

Kitty looked around. "Er, hello," she said hesitantly. "I'm Kitty. I hope you can help me. You see . . . I'm actually a girl. I turned into a cat last night for the first time ever. And I don't know why!"

An excited murmur traveled through the circle. "Another one!" breathed a little tortoiseshell next to Kitty.

"Well, you've come to the right place," Tiger told Kitty solemnly. "Our Guardian can help you."

All the cats nodded respectfully as the small black cat with the white patch stepped quietly into the circle. *So she is the Guardian. I was right!* thought Kitty.

"Welcome, Kitty," the Guardian meowed. "You have a very rare gift. The lucky humans who possess it can be wonderful friends to cats. In fact, I sense that you might even have what it takes to be our *new* Guardian."

"*New* Guardian?" asked Smoky, puzzled. "But what about——"

"I have decided to step down as Guardian of this Council," the black cat explained. The other cats gasped. "I am getting too old, but I had to wait until the right cat came along to take my place. Now, I believe she has."

Misty purred, excited for Kitty. But the other cats seemed upset. "B-but you've been our Guardian for years!" protested Biscuits. "What will we do without you, Suki?"

Suki! thought Kitty. *That's the same name as——*

Suki held up a paw, and the circle fell

quiet again. "I am sure Kitty will be an excellent Guardian," she said. "I know she is kind, thoughtful, and brave and will serve our Council well."

"But *how* do you know that?" asked Tiger curiously. "We've never met Kitty before."

Suki's eyes twinkled. "Because she's my granddaughter!" she announced proudly.

There were gasps around the circle. Kitty stared at the black cat in disbelief. *"Grandma?"*

Chapter 6

Finally Kitty understood why Suki had a collar like hers. "It's your necklace!" she exclaimed.

"I have waited a long time to tell you our secret," Grandma meowed happily. "The females in our family have had this special ability for hundreds of years. I became a cat for the first time when I was your age, so I knew you were ready!

But you *must* keep it a secret, Kitty. If any human finds out about your gift, the magic will be broken, and you will never be able to turn into a cat again."

"I understand," Kitty replied solemnly.

Grandma purred proudly. "Then you are on the right path to become our Cat Council's new Guardian!"

The rest of the circle had listened in silence, amazed. Now Kitty realized all the cats were purring together, a deep rumbling noise that she could almost feel in the grass under her paws. Grandma chuckled. "I think the Council approves," she whispered.

But something was bothering Kitty. "I'd love to become the Guardian," she said. "The trouble is, I don't know how to help cats with their problems. I'm still getting used to being a cat myself!"

"You will learn," Grandma reassured her. "You just have to trust both your human and cat hearts, Kitty. Listen to them, and you will be a wonderful Guardian. I promise."

Kitty thought of something else. "Each time I've turned into a cat, it was because I sneezed! Could it happen when I don't mean it to? Is there an easier way?"

Grandma nodded at the charm on Kitty's collar. "With practice, you will be able to turn into a cat and back whenever you want," she explained. "Just say the words."

Kitty felt dazed. There was so much to remember!

"Now it's time to make your Guardian Promise," Grandma told her. She held out her paw and asked Kitty to place her own paw on top. "Kitty, do you promise to protect and help all cats, whenever you can?"

"I promise," answered Kitty, feeling very serious.

"Then you may walk among catkind as one of them," declared Grandma.

Suddenly Kitty was surrounded by the whole Council, all purring happily and wanting to bump heads with her. It felt strange at first, but Kitty quickly understood they were doing it to be friendly, and she shyly bumped heads back. *I'm going to be the new Guardian!* she thought to herself, feeling a rush of amazed pride.

Misty was the last cat to rub heads with Kitty. "Well done, Kitty!" she meowed happily.

Grandma turned to Kitty. "I think your first task after becoming the new Guardian should be to help your friend Misty," she said. "I'll help you if you need it. But I have faith that you can find a way to make it right." She looked around the circle. "If we don't stop Fang and Claws soon, they'll take over the whole town!"

Chapter 7

It was a day later, and Kitty's parents had arrived home that morning from their trip, bringing back lots of new things for their shop. But Mom and Dad were both tired from their long journey. So, to Kitty's delight, they went to bed early that night. Grandma followed them upstairs, yawning loudly and winking at Kitty.

As soon as the house was quiet, she sprang out of bed and pushed her window open. She was going to try using the necklace to turn into a cat this time! Then she could go and see how Misty was getting on. Taking a deep breath, Kitty grasped the charm on her necklace and quietly read the words on it:

"Human hands to kitten paws,

Human fingers, kitten claws."

She closed her eyes as the tingling feeling shot through her body. When she opened them again, she'd turned back into a cat! And she hadn't even sneezed! Kitty felt pleased she was getting better at this, and she purred proudly. Then, with one easy leap, Kitty landed lightly on the window sill. From

here, she could jump down onto the kitchen roof and then into the yard. She hesitated for a second, the breeze ruffling her fur. It looked like a long way, but she knew she could do it!

Once her paws hit the grass, she bounced right onto the playhouse, then padded along the fence until she reached Jenny's garden. Misty was peering nervously through the cat flap. As soon as she saw Kitty, she jumped through.

"I came as soon as my family went to bed!" meowed Kitty. "Any sign of Fang and Claws?"

Misty shook her head. "No, thank goodness!" she replied—but as she spoke, Kitty felt her fur standing on end. She whirled around.

"I thought we told you this was *our* garden," sneered Fang, his cruel eyes narrowed. Beside him, Claws hissed threateningly. The Persians had crept up behind Kitty and Misty without them noticing!

"Kitty, quick! Let's go back inside!" whispered Misty fearfully.

Kitty shook her head. "You have to stand up to them," she said under her breath. "We can't let bullies get away with it."

Misty looked a little unsure, but with another encouraging meow from Kitty, she took a brave step forward. "S-stop being so unkind," Misty began. "You have your own yard to play in!"

Claws prowled closer to them. "Well, we want yours too," he hissed. "And you can't stop us!"

"That's where you're wrong," Kitty said, moving to stand next to Misty.

"Misty has friends here in the neighbor-hood. We won't let you push her around!" Kitty fluffed out her fur. She could sense Misty feeling more confident too.

"Yeah!" Misty added, looking Claws and Fang in the eyes. "Why don't you just go back to your own yard?"

Fang looked puzzled, then surprised. He glared at Misty. "Whatever, new cat. You just wait . . ." he hissed, but then he finally turned and jumped up onto the fence. "Come on, Claws," he said, slinking away. Claws let out one more growl before following his brother.

"You did it!" said Kitty happily, bumping her head against Misty's. "Well done!"

Misty purred gratefully. "At least they're gone for now," she said.

Kitty noticed movement on the fence. She saw a little black cat with a patch of white fur jump gracefully down into the garden.

"Well done, girls! Bullies are always caught unawares when you stand up to them. Let's hope they don't come back."

Kitty turned to her grandmother. "Thanks, Grandma. What are you doing here?" she asked.

"I was just taking a midnight stroll. It's my favorite time to be a cat!" Grandma replied, trotting toward the garden gate. "Why don't you and Misty join me on my walk, and I'll show you around?"

Kitty purred happily in agreement, and both she and Misty followed Grandma out the gate, down a quiet alleyway, and on to Willow Street, where Kitty's parents had their shop. Kitty was excited to be spending time with Grandma as a cat, especially as

Grandma pounced and ran through the streets!

"Keep up, kittens!" Grandma called, chuckling, as she raced along the top of a high wall.

As they padded along excitedly, Kitty noticed lots of curious, furry faces peering at them and smiling. "Good evening!" Grandma called out to cats as they ran past. "This is my granddaughter, Kitty, and her friend Misty, who's just moved to the neighborhood!"

"It feels like every cat in town must be out here, Grandma!" said Kitty, looking around. Cats were play-fighting in the street and even snoozing in the moonlight. She recognized a few of them from the Cat Council.

"Almost!" replied Grandma. "Cats love coming out at night when there are no humans around."

Suddenly, Kitty felt something drip on her head. "Oh, what's that?" she said, looking up.

Next to her, Misty let out a hiss. "Rain!" she meowed, sounding alarmed. "Quick! Get inside!"

Kitty giggled as all the cats began to race for cover, sheltering under trees and squeezing underneath cars. "It's only a little shower," she began. But when a second drop landed on her fur, she shuddered. "Oh! But it feels horrible!" she exclaimed, surprised.

"Let's go home," Grandma said, looking at the dark clouds gathering

above them. "It's going to pour. You'll soon find out there's nothing we cats hate more than getting wet!"

Kitty stared at Grandma. "Cats hate getting wet," she repeated. "Grandma, you're a genius. You've just given me a brilliant idea. I think I know how to make Fang and Claws go away for good!"

Chapter 8

The next day was Saturday, and Kitty rang Jenny's doorbell after lunch. She and Grandma had searched their shed that morning and found what they were looking for. Together, they'd carried the big cardboard box down the street to Jenny's house.

"Ooh, what's this?" asked Jenny's mom when she answered the door.

"My old wading pool!" Kitty explained. "Grandma and I wondered if Barney might like it? It's really fun to use on a warm day!"

"That's so kind of you. I'm sure Barney will love it!" replied Jenny's mom. "Why don't you come inside, and we can set it up in the garden?"

Kitty caught Grandma's eye and winked. This was exactly what she had hoped for. Everything was going according to plan so far!

Grandma left Kitty at Jenny's house, and Jenny's mom blew up the wading pool and filled it with water. Jenny and Kitty giggled as Barney squealed and splashed water everywhere happily. "He loves it!" said Kitty.

"I don't think Misty does, though," said Jenny, pointing. Misty was curled up in a patch of sun at the other end of the garden, eyeing the wading pool nervously.

"At least she's out in the garden today," Kitty said, smiling at the little cat. *Because she knows Fang and Claws won't come back with people around!* she thought. *But if my plan works, Misty won't have to worry about those terrible cats anymore.*

At the end of the afternoon, Jenny's mom lifted Barney out of the wading pool and wrapped him in a fluffy towel. "Time for dinner, then it's bedtime for this one!" she announced. "Kitty, your grandma has just called to say your dinner will be ready in ten minutes, so you'd better get home. Thanks again for the wading pool!"

"You're welcome!" replied Kitty, smiling.

Before she left, she nudged the wading pool just a little farther to the right. It had to be in the perfect spot for her plan to work—just underneath the fence . . .

After washing the dishes that evening, it was time for Kitty to put the next part of her plan into action.

"I think I've left my book in the backyard," she told her dad. "I'll just pop outside and look for it."

"Good luck, Kitty-cat!" whispered

Grandma as Kitty slipped out through the back door.

The sun had set, and the stars twinkled in a pretty, violet-colored sky. Making sure no one could see her, Kitty whispered the words on her necklace.

"Human hands to kitten paws,
Human fingers, kitten claws!"

As soon as Kitty had turned into a cat, she jumped onto the fence and ran along it until she reached Jenny's garden.

Misty was nowhere to be seen, and Kitty guessed that her friend was inside. She padded up to the cat flap, nudged it aside with her paw and meowed, "Misty?"

Misty was curled up on a kitchen chair. "I have a plan. Come outside!" Kitty whispered.

Misty seemed nervous and said that Claws and Fang had been prowling around earlier, but she jumped down from the chair and followed Kitty into the garden. Kitty explained her idea, but Misty was still not sure.

"Just remember how brave you were before," Kitty said encouragingly. "You can do it!"

Kitty hid behind a bush, and Misty waited on the lawn. Both of them listened for any unusual noises. Soon, Kitty's ears twitched as she heard two fluffy tails swishing closer, and then two white faces popped over the fence, staring down at Misty. Even Kitty felt a bit worried as Fang gave a nasty, mocking laugh.

"We told you we'd be back when your friend wasn't around to protect you!" he hissed.

"Now we're going to take over your garden for *good*," added Claws.

Kitty saw Misty take a deep breath. "No, you're not," she told the cats, shakily but firmly. "This is *my* garden and *my* home!"

The Persians shot each other an amused glance. "Oh, really?" meowed Claws slyly.

"Really!" said Misty, taking another step toward the fence. "If you don't go back to your own yard, you're going to regret it."

Kitty felt so proud, especially knowing how scared Misty must be! She held her breath as the Persians arched their backs and bared their sharp teeth. She hoped her plan would work! Just then, Fang hissed, "Let's get her!" and he and Claws sprang down together . . .

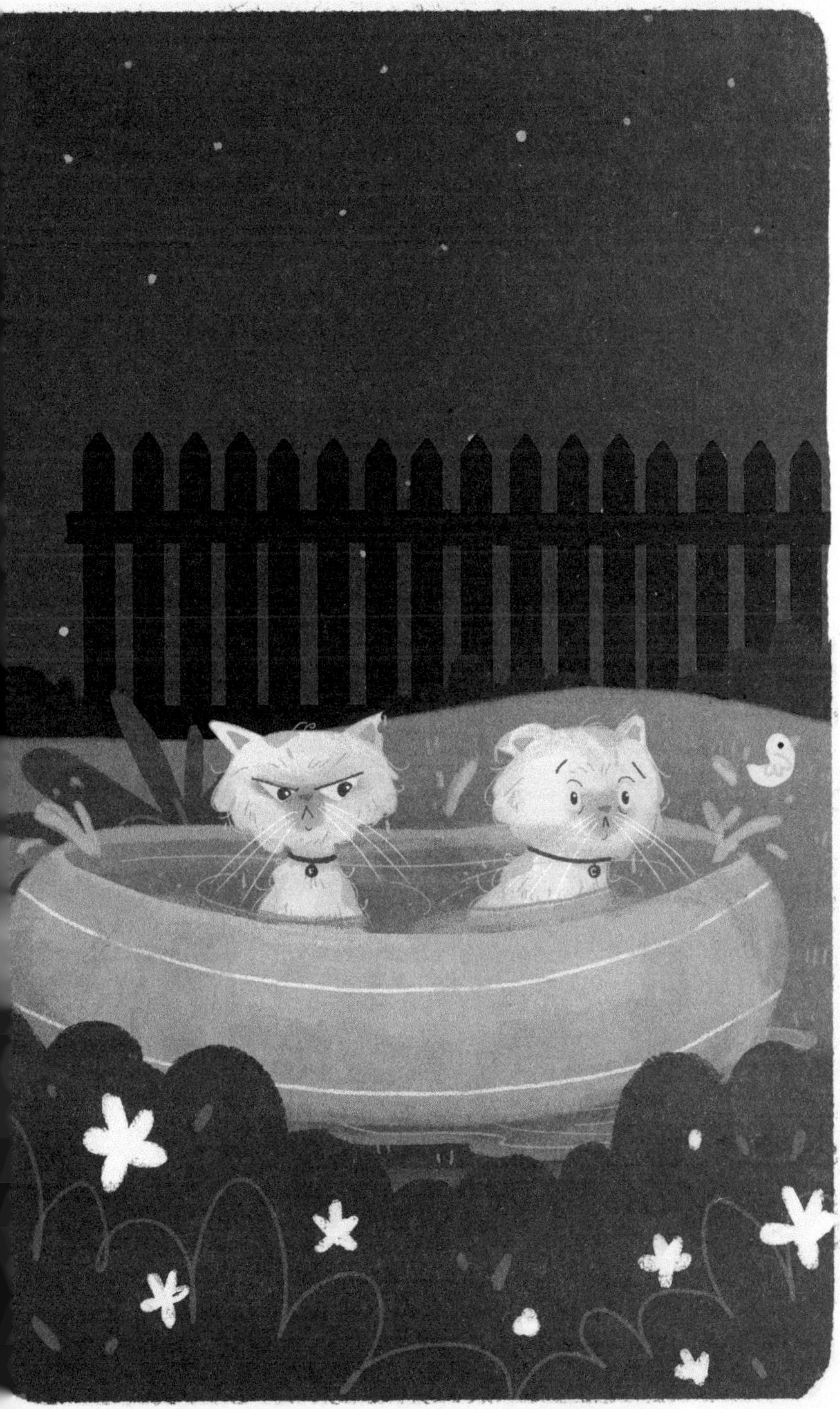

. . . and landed right in the wading pool with a huge splash!

"Water!" spluttered Fang, gasping in horror. His fluffy white fur was dripping wet and plastered to his body. "I HATE water!"

"It was a trap!" yowled Claws, scrambling out of the wading pool. "I don't want to come back to this yard any more, Fang!"

"Good!" shouted Misty, purring happily as the soggy cats ran away. "That's what you get for being bullies!"

"That was fabulous! You were so brave, Misty," said Kitty, rushing out from behind the bush and bumping heads happily with her friend. "Well done!"

"Thank you so much for your clever plan, Kitty," Misty replied. "Just wait until we tell the Cat Council! You're going to be an amazing Guardian!"

"Let's go and tell Grandma it worked!" said Kitty excitedly.

Kitty and Misty trotted along the fence and jumped down into Kitty's yard. Kitty felt as though she might burst with pride.

"I'd better change back to a girl before anyone spots us," she said to Misty.

Just as she finished reciting the magic words from her collar's charm, she heard Dad calling her name, and the back door opened. Dad and Grandma stepped outside together, and Kitty saw a look of relief flash over Grandma's face when she saw that Kitty had changed back in time.

"Kitty!" said Dad in surprise. "There you are! I was beginning to wonder what was taking so long. Did you find your book?"

"Err . . . not yet," answered Kitty. She looked down at Misty rubbing her furry head against her legs. "I was just playing with Misty."

"So this is Jenny's new cat! She's lovely, isn't she?" said Kitty's dad, bending down to stroke Misty, who purred happily. As her dad wasn't looking, Kitty flashed Grandma a big smile. *It worked!* she mouthed, and Grandma beamed back.

"Kitty, I've just realized something. You're not sneezing!" Dad exclaimed. "Do you think you've grown out of your allergy?"

Kitty grinned. "I must have!" she answered, tickling Misty under the chin. "And I'm going to spend lots more time with cats from now on!" She couldn't wait!

MEET

Kitty

Kitty is a little girl who can magically turn into a cat! She is the Guardian of the Cat Council.

Tiger

Tiger is a big, brave tabby tomcat. He is leader of the Cat Council.

Suki

Suki is Kitty's grandmother. She can magically turn into a cat too!

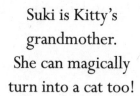

THE CATS

Misty

Misty is Kitty's best cat friend. She loves to play with her ball of wool.

Fang

Fang acts very tough but he hates to get wet.

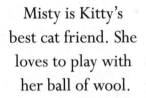

Claws

Claws is Fang's twin brother. He is missing a chunk of his left ear!

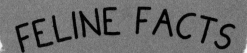

FELINE FACTS

Here are some
fun facts about our
purrrfect animal friends
that you might like
to know...

There are over
500 million pet
cats in the world!

Cats have **dreams**,
just like people do.

3.

Girl cats are called **"queens"** and boy cats are called **"toms."**

4.

Persian cats like **Fang** and **Claws** originated in Persia (modern-day Iran) over 500 years ago!

5.

A cat's night vision is **six times** more powerful than a human's.

Kitty's Magic

Shadow the Lonely Cat

Chapter 1

Kitty Kimura rushed out of the school gates with her best friend, Jenny. "Grandma said she'll be picking us up today," called Kitty. "Look, there she is!"

Kitty's grandmother was waiting for the girls with a smile on her face. Grandma was Japanese and, like her eight-year-old granddaughter, she had dark-colored eyes and shiny black hair—but Grandma's bob had a pure white streak running through it. She lived with Kitty and her parents, who ran a special shop selling Japanese gifts. It was Grandma who had given Kitty her nickname. Kitty's *real* name was Koemi, but hardly anybody called her that.

"Hello, girls!" Grandma said. "How was school today?"

As they walked home, Kitty and Jenny told Grandma their news.

"Our teacher, Ms. Brookes, says we're starting a special project soon, where we do something to help the community," Kitty explained. "Every year her class does something different. Last year they picked up litter in the park."

"We all have to think of ideas and give them to Ms. Brookes," added Jenny. "Then she'll pick the best one."

"I'm sure you girls will think of something," Grandma told them.

"Kitty, why don't you come over to my house this week?" Jenny said. "We could try to think of an idea then, and play with Misty!" Misty was Jenny's cat, a pretty silver tabby with blue eyes.

"Good idea!" Kitty told her friend, grinning.

Jenny continued chatting excitedly, describing how cute it was when Misty leaped at the point of light from the new laser pen she'd gotten. But what Jenny didn't realize was that Kitty already knew about it. Someone else had told her the night before: Misty herself!

Kitty had a *very* special secret.

Just a few weeks ago, Kitty had discovered something amazing about herself. She'd always believed she was allergic to cats, but one day Grandma had given her an unusual present: a beautiful necklace with a silver pendant engraved with a picture of a cat on the front and some mysterious words on the back.

That night, Kitty had gone to a sleepover at Jenny's house. When Jenny was fast asleep, with Misty curled up close by, Kitty had sneezed an especially powerful sneeze. When she opened her eyes, she was no longer a girl—she had turned into a cat!

Even better, she learned that all cats could talk to each other. Misty had quickly become her very best cat friend, and Kitty was getting to know lots of other cats in town too. She was still getting used to her incredible gift. It turned out that the special words written on her necklace could help Kitty control when she turned into a cat, if she needed to. Kitty knew she had to be careful that nobody else learned about her ability, because if her secret got out the magic would be broken forever.

Kitty and Jenny skipped ahead of Grandma, but as they turned the next corner, Kitty realized her friend was slowing down. "What's wrong?" she asked.

Jenny pointed up ahead of them. "Mrs. Thornton's house is so spooky," she said.

Kitty looked up the path lined with crooked old trees that led up to a big house at the top of a small, steep hill. The yard had a huge tree with twisted branches. It was full of tall, tangled, overgrown weeds, the black paint on the front door was peeling, and three of the windows were cracked. "I know!" Kitty replied, shivering. "My mom says she used to see Mrs. Thornton shopping in town, but no one's seen her around recently. She's really old."

"Some of the kids in our class say she's a witch," added Jenny, eyeing the house nervously. "She has a black cat

called Shadow, and they say he's a witch's cat. Look—he's over there!"

Kitty caught a glimpse of wild dark fur and glinting eyes among the weeds. Shadow was crouched low, and Kitty could only just make him out. She remembered having met him once, but during all the nights she'd spent wandering around town in her cat form, she hadn't bumped into Shadow since.

She tried to call him over, but Shadow turned away, darting through the bushes. Kitty saw the broken cat flap on the front door swinging as he rushed inside. *He obviously wants to stay close to home,* she thought.

After Kitty and Grandma had dropped Jenny off at home and walked along the street to their own house, Kitty decided to ask Grandma if she knew why they hadn't seen Shadow much lately. After all, Grandma was the perfect person to ask about any cat in town—because Kitty wasn't the only human who could turn into a cat. Grandma had the very same gift!

"Grandma, do you know anything about Shadow, the black cat who lives with Mrs. Thornton?" she asked.

Grandma paused. "Shadow?" she said. "Let me think. He used to come to our Cat Council meetings all the time, but recently he's been keeping to himself. He tends to stay in his own house or yard."

The Cat Council was a special

gathering of cats from all over town, which met at night and helped cats with their problems. Kitty and Misty were the newest members of the Cat Council, and Kitty had an extra-special role. She had been chosen to take over from Grandma as the Guardian, the leader of the Council! Kitty was very proud to be the Guardian and had promised to do the best job she could. "So Shadow hasn't always been like this?" she said.

Grandma glanced at Kitty and smiled. "Why are you asking, Kitty?" she said.

Kitty nodded. "There must be a reason for Shadow behaving differently," she said. "Maybe he needs some help?"

Chapter 2

After dinner that evening, Kitty's mom explained that she and Dad were traveling to Chicago the next morning to visit a special fair selling Japanese objects. They were hoping to find some unusual ornaments to stock in their shop.

Mrs. Kimura bent down to give Kitty a goodnight kiss. "Grandma will take you to school and pick you up, okay, sweetheart?"

"Okay!" replied Kitty, trying not to sound too eager. Once her parents had gone to bed, Kitty knew that she would be free to change into a cat without risking being seen. Then she could start finding out what was going on with Shadow and whether she could help.

Kitty waited for her parents' bedroom door to close and then counted to a hundred. Soon everything was still, and she was sure they must have fallen asleep. As quietly as she could, Kitty opened her bedroom window, and then, very quietly, she whispered the words that were also etched onto the back of the pendant on her necklace.

"Human hands to kitten paws,
Human fingers, kitten claws."

Right away, a strange fizzing, tickling feeling began. Kitty grinned as it swept through her feet and legs, then her tummy and arms, right up to the top of her head and the tips of her fingers. She closed her eyes and waited for the feeling to stop, took a deep breath, and opened her eyes.

Kitty always thought it was funny how much bigger her cozy little bedroom seemed once she was in her cat form. Her bed towered above her, and her animal posters and photographs of Jenny and Misty seemed miles away. She lifted a fuzzy black front leg and giggled to see a small, furry, white-tipped paw with tiny claws. She let out an excited little mew and looked back to see her long furry tail swish behind her. She shook out her whiskers and trotted around the rug on her bedroom floor, thrilled to be back

in her cat form. *This is so amazing*, she
thought to herself. *I'm not sure I'll ever get
used to it!*

Kitty crouched low against the
carpet, then sprang into the air, landing
lightly on the windowsill. She caught

sight of her reflection in the window: a small black face with neat little ears, bright green eyes, a black nose, and whiskers. Around her neck was a collar with a silver pendant. Kitty's necklace also changed when she became a cat!

She breathed in the amazing mixture of smells from outside: freshly cut grass, flowers, Grandma's herb patch, and the scent of several cats, including Misty's scent and her own. Kitty's sense of smell was much stronger when she turned into a cat—and so was her ability to see in the dark. It was one of the things she loved best about her gift.

With a little wriggle, she crouched low, then used her strong back legs to jump straight out the window. She landed on the kitchen roof, then leaped the rest of the way down into the yard. She trotted through the grass, getting used to working her four furry little legs together, then sprang up onto the roof of her playhouse, then hopped onto the back fence. With her tail arched for extra balance and her claws gripping the wood, she could run along easily. And Kitty knew exactly where she wanted to head first: Shadow's house.

It was dark now, though, and as she neared Mrs. Thornton's house, the path grew very quiet. Although Kitty's sharp eyes could see in the gloom, she still felt a little bit nervous. *I wish I'd asked Misty to come along*, she thought, as her heartbeat started to quicken.

Kitty padded slowly up to the front gate and peered through it. She could just make out the gleam of a pair of eyes and realized that Shadow was crouched on the steps in front of the door. Kitty meowed to say hello. "My name's Kitty," she said, as cheerfully as she could manage. "I think we met at the Cat Council once, but I don't think I've seen you there lately. Is everything all right?"

There was a silence, then Kitty heard a low growl. She had already learned that this was a very unfriendly noise for cats to make, so she hesitated. Should she try again?

"It must be a bit quiet living all the way up here, away from the town

without any other cats to talk to. Maybe if you came out to—" Kitty began, but she jumped as Shadow's growl became a nasty hiss.

"No!" he meowed quickly. "I'm not leaving my yard again."

Kitty frowned. What did that mean? Why was Shadow being so unfriendly? She trotted away from his house a little, not sure what to do. Then Kitty spotted three small scratch marks in a tree trunk close by. They made a triangle shape, and she knew this mark was important. It was the sign that another neighborhood cat had called a meeting of the Cat Council. Someone else might need her help!

Suddenly, in the distance, Kitty heard

several cats meowing a special call out into the night air. They were all voices she recognized as being part of the Cat Council. The meeting was about to start!

"Listen," she said, turning and trotting back the way she came. "I'm going to the Cat Council meeting right now.

Why don't you come along? It's a lovely warm night. You could stretch your legs and—"

"Go away!" said Shadow. "I'm staying right here!"

Kitty decided that for now, it was better not to make Shadow even more upset or angry. She turned and trotted back down the hill, heading in the direction of the woods where the Cat Council always met. *I'll leave Shadow alone for the moment*, she thought. *But hopefully I'll be able to find out what's wrong soon. I just need to figure out a way to get him to talk to me!*

Chapter 3

Kitty ran through the dark wood and headed toward the clearing, where a group of cats were gathering together in a circle. Kitty spotted Tiger, the rather bossy but kind old tomcat who led the Cat Council, perched in between a glamorous British Shorthair called Coco and a friendly gray cat named Smoky. Other cats were still arriving from all directions, meowing hello and trotting to their places.

"Hi, Kitty!" called Misty as Kitty padded up to the circle. Kitty meowed a greeting to everyone and said hello to those nearby, including her friend, by gently bumping heads with them. Then Kitty trotted to her place next to a small black cat with a white patch on her head—Grandma in her cat form!

"I think that's everyone tonight! Let's start by saying the Meow Vow," suggested Tiger.

Together, the cats recited the special words that started every meeting of the Cat Council:

"We promise now,
 This solemn vow,

To help somehow,
When you meow."

Tiger nodded once the Vow was finished. "Now, which cat called today's meeting?" he asked, looking round.

A fluffy young tortoiseshell stepped into the circle. Kitty noticed she was walking with a slight limp, placing one paw down on the ground very carefully. "My name is Bella," the cat said to introduce herself.

"Welcome, Bella," replied Tiger. "Do you have a problem to share with us? Kitty here is going to be taking over as our Guardian. She might be able to give you some advice." He gestured with a paw to show Bella where Kitty was sitting.

Kitty nodded at Bella, hoping that she'd be able to help. "Yes! Tell us what the problem is, and I'll definitely do my best," she meowed warmly. She knew how coming to the Cat Council for the first time could make a cat feel nervous and tried her best to make new cats feel at ease. It wasn't so long ago that she'd been new too!

"Well, I'm having problems with my human, Max," Bella explained.

"Is he unkind to you?" asked a little white kitten named Poppy, blinking worriedly.

"No, Max is a lovely human," replied Bella. "But recently, he's been putting these funny white things in my food! They're small and round, a bit like tiny pebbles. They taste funny too. I want to ask you all, how I can avoid eating them?"

Kitty giggled to herself. She knew exactly what the white things must be—medicine! She had watched a show on TV about vets and had seen them doing the exact same thing, hiding pills inside bowls of animals' food.

But the rest of the Council had a very different reaction to Bella's story—and before Kitty could say anything, they were all giving Bella their own suggestions! "You must do everything you can not to eat the pebbles!" announced Tiger loudly. "Hide them under your paws until your human goes away. Then push them under the sofa or the doormat— somewhere he won't notice them!"

"Or you could *pretend* to eat them," added Smoky seriously. "Keep them hidden in your cheek and then spit them out when Max isn't looking."

"Just refuse," said Coco airily. "My human can never force me to do anything I don't want to. She knows I'm the boss in our house! If I were you, Bella, I would simply hiss and spit until your human stops putting the nasty things in your bowl. That ought to do the trick!"

Kitty decided it was time to jump in. "Bella, I think you *should* eat them," she said.

The other cats turned to look at her.

"What do you mean?" asked Bella, puzzled, but Grandma nodded encouragingly at Kitty.

"They're not pebbles, you see. They're medicine," explained Kitty. "Special things to make you better when you're sick. Have you felt bad recently, Bella?"

Bella cocked her head to one side

thoughtfully. "Well, I *do* have a sore paw," she admitted. "I scratched it on a thorn in the garden. It's very painful, and I've been limping ever since!"

"I think Max is giving you medicine to help your paw heal," Kitty told her. "It might not taste very good, but I promise that he wouldn't add it to your food unless you really needed it. You won't have to take it for long—just until your paw feels better."

There was a murmur around the circle, and Bella looked impressed. "Gosh, I had no idea!" she meowed. "Well, I'll give it a try. Thank you."

Grandma gave a proud purr.

"Well done, Kitty!" Misty said. "None of us normal cats would have known that."

"That's right! Because you're human too, you've got all sorts of extra knowledge to help us cats out," added Smoky. "That's what makes you such a good Guardian!"

Kitty purred happily as the rest of

the Council nodded. She always felt happy when she was able to solve a problem for one of her new cat friends.

"Now, does anyone have any other problems they need help with?" asked Tiger, looking around the circle.

Kitty stepped forward. "Actually, I wanted to ask you all about a cat called Shadow," she meowed. "I'm sure lots of you know him, but he hasn't come to a Council meeting for a long time. In fact, he refuses to leave his yard. I want to see if I can get Shadow to tell me what's wrong."

The rest of the Council hesitated. "I don't think there's anything *wrong* with Shadow. He just seems old and grumpy to me," Coco said, licking a paw.

Kitty couldn't argue with that. He did seem a bit moody. "Does anyone know if he's had any problems recently?"

The cats looked at one another, shaking their heads.

"I knew Shadow when we were both kittens, no bigger than young Poppy here," said Pinky, an old Sphynx cat. Kitty always thought Pinky was really interesting, because she was a breed of cat that didn't have any fur! "He used to be a friendly cat," Pinky continued. "He'd play with the leaves in the park with us, he'd help us chase away that nasty fox that used to lurk around the town square . . . But lately he refuses to leave his human's yard."

Kitty frowned. "I wonder what changed?"

"Shadow's scary!" piped up little Poppy, shivering. "I went exploring near his house one day. It's creepy, and he just seems to hide in the dark up there."

Kitty agreed that it was gloomy and overgrown up at Shadow's house. She'd felt a bit nervous there herself. But that didn't mean they shouldn't try to help him, did it?

But the other cats didn't seem to think it was worth it. "I think it's best to leave Shadow alone," Tiger said to the group. "It seems to me that he prefers being by himself."

Soon after that, Tiger announced that the meeting was over. Kitty felt disappointed. Something must have happened to make Shadow change. Even if he didn't want to come out and play with the other cats, surely they should try to get to the bottom of why he was behaving in such an unfriendly way? Kitty was new to being the Guardian, but she was certain that she should try to do something. There was a cat that needed her help!

Chapter 4

The next day, Kitty went to Jenny's house after school. "We can play with Misty and the laser pen!" Jenny said as they dropped their backpacks by the front door. "Let's go and find her."

Misty was curled up in the sunshine on the kitchen windowsill, and she jumped straight down with a happy meow when she saw the girls come in.

Jenny found the laser pen and switched
it on, pointing the beam at the wall.
Kitty giggled as Misty leaped at it,
swiping the tiny circle of light excitedly
with her paws. Jenny waved the pen
around the kitchen and Misty darted

under chairs as she chased the light. "See, she loves it!" exclaimed Jenny.

Kitty grinned, remembering how excited Misty had been when she described the game. When Jenny went to answer the phone in the hallway, Kitty crouched down and whispered to Misty, "That does look like a lot of fun! Sometimes I wish I had my own human to play with when I turn into a cat—then I'd be able to join in games like that too!"

Misty purred in agreement and rubbed her furry head against Kitty's ankles. Kitty knew that Misty could still understand everything she said, like all cats could understand humans. Kitty could only understand Misty's cat sounds when she was a cat herself, though.

As Jenny came back into the kitchen, Kitty quickly stopped talking.

"That was your grandma on the phone! She says your dinner's ready," Jenny explained. "See you at school tomorrow? Maybe we'll come up with a good idea for our community project then. I still haven't thought of anything!"

Kitty ate her spaghetti very quickly—so quickly that Grandma chuckled as she took her last bite. "You're in a hurry tonight, Kitty!" she said, smiling. "I bet I can guess why."

Kitty grinned. "I want to change into a cat again this evening!" she explained. "I thought with Mom and Dad still being away, I could use the chance to go out a bit earlier. Would that be okay?"

"I don't see why not," Grandma told her. "Just be careful while you're out and about."

"I will," promised Kitty, and then she remembered something. "Grandma, I was thinking about Shadow. It seems a shame that nobody at the Cat Council wanted to find out why he won't come out of his yard, don't you think? I know he's grumpy, but maybe he's unhappy. I really want to think of a way to help him."

Grandma smiled at Kitty. "That, my dear, is why you will make such a wonderful Guardian," she said. "You're always looking to help. I'm sure you'll figure out if there's anything you can help him with soon enough." Grandma gave Kitty's hand a squeeze.

Kitty quickly put her plate in the sink and slipped out into the backyard. This was a safe place to change into a cat because it was sheltered from all the neighboring houses by tall trees and bushes. Quietly she spoke the words she needed to change shape and closed her eyes as the bubbling, fizzing feeling swept through her. It was so fantastic, every time!

When she opened her eyes again, every blade of grass around her seemed clearer and greener, and she could hear the sound of a tiny butterfly fluttering its wings right at the other end of the yard. She gave a happy meow and flexed her

tail. She paused to give her white-tipped paws and legs a quick clean, swiping her paws over her quivering whiskers quickly too. She was still getting used to having all that soft, fuzzy black fur!

Kitty's cat ears pricked up as the back door opened behind her, and

Grandma stepped outside. She bent down to give Kitty's head a gentle stroke and tickle the fur on her back.

"Have fun!" Grandma whispered.

Kitty purred happily, then jumped up onto the back fence and trotted along it until she reached the street. It was a lovely spring evening, and Kitty enjoyed being in cat form while it was still a little bit light outside.

As she padded along, past Jenny's house and around the next corner, she caught a glimpse of tortoiseshell fur ahead of her. The cat turned and Kitty realized it was Bella, the young cat who had come to the Cat Council meeting and asked about the little white pills her human was hiding in her food bowl.

"Bella!" meowed Kitty, and the two cats bumped their foreheads together in a friendly greeting.

"I ate my medicine up today, just like you said," Bella told Kitty proudly. "And my sore paw is already feeling a lot better! So I've come out to play! Let's go and see if we can find a mouse to catch!" the little cat suggested eagerly, giving an excited leap and then racing off down the street.

Kitty wasn't sure she liked that idea very much. The thought of it made her tummy feel a bit funny! Even so, she ran after Bella and quickly caught up. As the cats began to trot down the next street, Kitty suddenly felt an odd prickling feeling along her back. Without even

meaning to, she had pricked up her ears and was crouching close to the ground. Bella was doing the same, and letting out a low growl.

What's going on? Kitty wondered, glancing around.

Suddenly she spotted what was making her behave so strangely. Walking down the street from the other direction were a young man and his fierce-looking German Shepherd!

The dog narrowed his mean black eyes as he spotted the cats. He lurched straight forward, pulling hard on his leash, and the man had to struggle to keep hold of the other end. "Nipper, stop it!" he shouted.

The dog took no notice, but opened his mouth and began to bark loudly, revealing a glimpse of sharp white teeth. As he pulled forward, the young man began to stumble and dropped the

leash. Bella let out a frightened hiss and darted away, but Kitty felt frozen to the spot. She stared in horror as the German Shepherd broke free and began thundering down the street, heading straight toward her!

Chapter 5

As the growling dog ran toward Kitty, she finally managed to move her paws again. She turned and raced down the street, darting as quickly as she could past lampposts and parked cars. Behind her, she could hear the German Shepherd barking noisily and the man yelling for him to stop.

I've got to hide! Kitty thought

desperately, picturing those horrible
sharp teeth. She took the next left and
ran up a steep hill. It was only when she
was halfway up it, dodging past tangled
weeds and patches of nettles, that
she realized she was heading straight
toward Mrs. Thornton's house. The
cracked dark windows and shabby front

door came into view, and as Kitty ducked under the fence, hoping the dog wouldn't be able to squeeze his body through it, she almost ran headfirst into another cat—Shadow! He yowled in surprise.

"What are you doing here again?" he meowed. "And what's all that noise?"

"I'm really sorry, I didn't mean to startle you!" panted Kitty. "But I was running away from—"

Before she could finish, the German Shepherd charged up the hill after Kitty. He growled noisily as he reached the fence and spotted not one, but *two* cats on the other side. He ran from one end of the fence to the other, barking

in frustration as he scrabbled at the wood and searched for a way into the yard.

Shadow hissed, arching his back and tail, and both cats took several quick steps back. Kitty couldn't help trembling in fright.

"That nasty dog's going to wake up

my human with all his barking!" Shadow said anxiously.

"Sorry, Shadow," Kitty whispered. "He just chased me up here. Look, his human's here now. I really hope he can get hold of him!" She'd never run into a dog in her cat form—it was petrifying!

"Nipper!" she heard the young man shout. "Come here! Bad dog! No treats for you tonight!"

As the man tried to grab hold of his dog's leash, the German Shepherd continued to jump against the fence. Suddenly Kitty found herself giving a terrified squeal—the dog had managed to push through one of the wooden posts and leap through the gap into the yard!

"Nipper, no!" shouted the young man, as the dog ran straight for Kitty. She turned and raced toward the nearest tree, pouncing up the trunk, and crouched, shaking, in the highest branches. The German Shepherd tried to jump up after her, but he was much too heavy—so instead, he turned and fixed his gaze on Shadow!

At last, the man managed to grab hold of his dog's leash and wrap it firmly around his hand three times. "Got you!" he said, sounding very relieved. "We're going straight home. Bad dog!" With a jerk on the leash, he led the German Shepherd out of Mrs. Thornton's yard and down the hill.

Kitty felt herself slowly start to

relax. The arch in her back began to drop, and the horrid pricking feeling in her fur started to disappear. She peered down through the leaves from the branch she was perched on. Shadow called up to her. "Kitty, you can come down now!" he meowed. "That horrible dog and his human have gone."

Kitty tried to find her footing to make her way down from the tree, but suddenly she felt unsure. "I-I don't think I can come down, Shadow!" she called. "I've never climbed this high up in a tree before. I think I'm stuck!" She looked down helplessly at the older black cat, starting to feel frightened again.

"It's okay, Kitty," Shadow said, his meow sounding more reassuring now.

"I'll help you climb down. I go up into that tree all the time!"

Kitty was grateful that Shadow was there to help her, but she felt bad—as the Guardian, she had hoped to help *him*!

"Now, you see that branch a little way below you, off to the right?" Shadow asked, sitting under the tree and looking up at Kitty. Kitty nodded, a bit too scared to meow back. "Shuffle backward a bit toward the tree trunk, then jump down onto that branch. I promise, it's nice and strong. Use your tail for balance," Shadow called.

Kitty took a deep breath and then did as he'd explained. She made it!

"Well done, Kitty!" Shadow said. "Now, just one more branch—can you see the one just below you? I left my claw marks on it a long time ago, so that I know which branch to use when I climb down. Jump onto there, and then you'll be able to make the leap down to the ground easily."

"I'm not sure . . ." Kitty began. The ground still seemed so far away.

Shadow let out an encouraging purr. "You can do it!"

Kitty swallowed, then jumped down again onto the branch Shadow had scratched. He was right! Now the ground seemed much closer. With a little meow, she made the next jump and was relieved to feel the grass under her paws again.

"Thank you so much, Shadow!" Kitty said with a relieved purr, bumping heads happily with the older cat without even thinking. Shadow seemed to

hesitate a moment, but then returned
her head bump too.

"That's okay," he said.

Suddenly, an eerie-sounding creak came from behind her. Oh no! Even though things were a bit friendlier with Shadow now, Kitty couldn't help being worried about Mrs. Thornton catching her in the yard. What if she was as scary as the kids at school said? Should she run away? But then, what would Shadow think? They'd only just begun to make friends, and Kitty still wanted to help him if she could. Planting her paws and trying to be brave, Kitty watched as the front door of the spooky old house began to open . . .

Chapter 6

Kitty felt her whiskers tremble nervously. She knew deep down that the spooky rumors about Mrs. Thornton were just silly stories—there was no such thing as a *real* witch, after all. Even so, she was a bit worried.

Kitty held her breath as a frail, shaky voice called out, "Shadow? Shadow, sweetheart!" Then a figure appeared on the front step and peered into the garden. Mrs. Thornton had curly white hair, wore glasses on a long gold chain around her neck, and held a walking stick in front of her. She was surprisingly small and moved very slowly.

"There you are, sweetheart," she said, sounding relieved as Shadow trotted quickly over to her. He purred loudly, rubbing himself against her ankles. Kitty couldn't help feeling happy—and a bit jealous, like she did with Misty—about how much Shadow obviously loved his human. Mrs. Thornton clearly loved Shadow too. She smiled happily and bent down gingerly to scratch the soft fur under his chin, leaning heavily on her walking stick. "You like that, don't you, sweetheart," she said, and Shadow purred even louder, rolling onto his back as Mrs. Thornton laughed. But then she noticed Kitty.

"Oh, who's this?" asked Mrs. Thornton, reaching to put on her glasses and smiling. "You've met another cat, have you, Shadow?"

Kitty stepped forward cautiously.

"It's okay, lovely!" She made kissing noises, and Kitty came closer. Mrs. Thornton bent down to rub Kitty's head too, and Kitty gave a happy purr of her own. "What a sweet little thing." She looked around the yard. "I thought I heard barking out here," she said. "I hope you two are all right. It's nice that you have a new friend, Shadow. I can't

remember the last time someone came to visit."

She straightened up from stroking Kitty and looked around with a sad expression on her face. "Maybe it's for the best. I'm rather embarrassed at how untidy my yard looks. It wasn't always like this, full of horrid weeds and brambles, was it? You used to lie out in the sun while I worked, didn't you, sweetheart?"

Shadow wound around her ankles again as she spoke. Kitty could tell he was hoping to cheer her up, but Mrs. Thornton sighed and finally murmured, "I just can't manage it since I fell and hurt my leg."

She smiled down at Shadow. "Never

mind, eh? I'm going back inside, darling," Mrs. Thornton said, and then turned back to Kitty. "You're welcome back whenever you like, little one!"

Kitty purred again. She was no longer afraid of Mrs. Thornton's house. Now that she had met the old lady and seen how friendly she really was, it didn't feel spooky anymore. But she knew she had to get home, or Grandma would start to worry. Mrs. Thornton went inside, leaving Shadow and Kitty alone in the garden.

"Your human is so lovely!" Kitty meowed happily to Shadow.

"She's the best," Shadow agreed shyly. "I've been very worried about her lately. I haven't wanted to leave her alone since she had her fall, even though I've been so lonely here without any cats to play with."

Kitty saw how sad Shadow was. "Let

me help you!" she said. "I'm the Guardian now and I'm sure——"

"There's nothing you can do," Shadow interrupted gloomily before disappearing into the house, his tail drooping sadly behind him.

With Shadow gone, Kitty made her way home quickly.

When Kitty trotted into the living room, Grandma was sipping a cup of green tea and reading a book. She looked up with a smile. "Hello there, Kitty cat!"

Kitty meowed the words to change back into her human form, knowing it was okay to do it in front of Grandma.

"Kitten paws to human toes,
Kitten whiskers, human nose."

She closed her eyes as the tingling

sensation swept over her furry body, and soon enough, she was looking down at her two hands, two feet, and the summer dress she'd been wearing that day!

She turned to Grandma quickly. "Guess what? I met Shadow, and Mrs. Thornton!"

She explained what she'd learned about the old lady's hurt leg. "I saw how much Shadow loves his human. I think he won't leave the house or garden because he's afraid she'll be left by herself and have another fall, but that just means he's lonely up there too." She finished, "I want to call another Cat Council for tomorrow evening. There has to be a way for us to help Shadow, *and* Mrs. Thornton."

Grandma smiled. "I think that's a very good idea, Kitty," she said. "I'm very proud of you. You're proving to be such a good Guardian already!"

Before Kitty went to bed, she quickly changed back into her cat form and slipped out onto the main street again. She padded up to a fence post and used her claws to scratch the special triangle symbol into the wood, then rubbed her fur against it. She gave a loud meow, so that any cats nearby would hear. Now the message would start to spread, and soon the rest of the cats in town would know that a meeting had been called for tomorrow night!

The next night Kitty waited until her parents were fast asleep before excitedly turning into her cat form. She leapt through the open bathroom window this time and landed with a soft thud on the roof of her parents' car. She trotted quickly along the street in the direction of the woods for the Cat Council meeting. Kitty couldn't wait to tell the other cats what she'd learned. Once everyone understood why Shadow had been behaving so strangely, she was sure they'd want to help him.

Soon Kitty was at the clearing, where the other cats of the Council were starting to gather. Once everyone was sitting in their places, and Tiger had led the cats in reciting the Meow Vow, he nodded at Kitty.

Kitty padded right into the middle of the circle. "Thank you all for coming," she meowed. "I wanted to tell you all that I found out why Shadow has been acting so oddly recently."

The other cats' ears pricked up

with curiosity as Kitty explained about Mrs. Thornton's fall. "Shadow and Mrs. Thornton love each other very much," she told them. "Shadow's not really unfriendly—he just doesn't want to leave his yard because he wants to stay at home to protect his human."

Around the circle, many furry heads were nodding. "I can understand that!" purred a fluffy gray Persian with a sparkly collar. "My human looks after me and gives me cuddles every day. I would want to look after her too, if she was in trouble."

Some of the other cats began to look at one another guiltily.

"I think because I don't have a human of my own, it took me a while to realize it," Kitty said. "Shadow is a little bit grumpy, but he's really nice deep down. He's just so worried about keeping Mrs. Thornton company, he's ended up all alone at the top of the hill."

"Oh dear," said Tiger, shaking his furry head. "I suppose we might have had the wrong impression about Shadow after all. Maybe we should have tried harder to find out what was wrong."

Pinky curled her skinny, long tail around her, and Kitty could tell she felt bad about Shadow too. "Well done for finding out what happened, Kitty," she meowed. "You're such a good Guardian!"

Grandma led the other cats in meows of agreement.

"But how are we going to help Shadow, Kitty?" asked a plump tabby.

"If Shadow doesn't want to leave his yard to come to us," said Kitty, "then we'll go to him! We're going to pay him a visit, right now."

A ripple of surprise went through the circle. "To that scary house?" asked Poppy nervously, her blue eyes very wide.

"Don't worry. You'll see when we get there that it's not that scary at all!" Kitty reassured her. "Come on— everyone follow me."

If any human had happened to glance out of their window that night, they would have seen an unusual sight: a long line of cats marching one by one down the street! Kitty led them up the

hill and into Mrs. Thornton's tangled yard. "Shadow?" she meowed. "It's me—Kitty! And I've brought lots of friends with me!"

At first, Shadow was a little startled by how many cats were strolling through his yard—but as they said hello, he began to bump heads with them, timidly at first, then growing more confident.

"This is fantastic!" he meowed to Kitty, purring happily as he watched some of the cats begin to chase after insects and play-fight with one another.

Kitty and Misty decided to start a game of hide-and-seek, and Shadow quickly showed them all how many fun places there were to hide in the wild, overgrown yard.

"I've missed playing!" he meowed cheerfully. "I've been so worried about my human that I just haven't felt like it."

Kitty bumped heads with Shadow. "See?" she meowed. "You've got lots of friends here—you don't have to be lonely. Just ask whenever you want someone to play with, okay? Or for anything!"

Shadow purred his agreement. "Thank you, Kitty," he said.

"And we promise not just to assume you want to be by yourself!" Kitty added. "Now we just need to think of a way to help your human too. And I think I've got an idea . . ."

Chapter 7

The next morning, Kitty couldn't wait to get to school. "Why are we rushing, Kitty?" asked her mom, chuckling as Kitty practically sprinted the last few steps into the playground. "Do you have a class you're really excited about?"

"I just need to talk to Jenny. It's important!" explained Kitty, reaching up to kiss her mom goodbye. Then she caught sight of Jenny's blond hair. "Oh look, there she is! See you tonight, Mom!"

Kitty raced over to meet Jenny. "Guess where I was last night!" she said.

Jenny guessed the movies, the swimming pool, and the ice rink before giving up. "I was at that house at the top of the hill—the one belonging to Mrs. Thornton!" explained Kitty.

Jenny stared at her friend. "But *why* would you go up there? It's so spooky!" she replied.

As the bell rang and the girls walked into their classroom together, Kitty told Jenny that she'd gone for a walk

after dinner and noticed a cat stuck up a tree in Mrs. Thornton's yard. She had already planned that part of the story, because she knew she couldn't tell Jenny the truth—that *she* had been the cat in the tree in Shadow's yard—without revealing her secret and losing her magic! "I . . . um . . . got some help getting the cat down," she continued, "and I ended up meeting Mrs. Thornton. She was a *really* nice lady. She seemed lonely, living up there all by herself. And she had a bad fall a few months ago, so that's why her house and yard look so wild and scary. It's because she can't look after them anymore."

"Oh no, that's so sad," said Jenny, pulling a face. "Kitty, I feel awful for saying her house was scary now."

"Well, I've thought of a way we can help her!" Kitty replied. "Remember Ms. Brookes's special project? She said we had to come up with an idea that would help the community. What if our class went and tidied up Mrs. Thornton's yard for her? We could pull up the weeds, sweep up the dead leaves, and plant some lovely new flowers for her. Maybe some of the teachers or parents could mend her broken windows and give her front door a fresh coat of paint. I'm sure she'd love having visitors up there as well."

Jenny's face lit up. "Kitty, that's a brilliant idea!"

"Let's hope Ms. Brookes likes it," replied Kitty. "Come on—let's go and ask her."

One week later, Kitty grinned proudly as she led her class up the hill toward

Mrs. Thornton's house, clutching a tray of daffodil bulbs in one hand and a little trowel in the other.

Ms. Brookes had *loved* Kitty's idea. In fact, she'd liked it so much that she had gone to pay Mrs. Thornton a visit that very same day. Mrs. Thornton had been delighted with Kitty's suggestion, and the next morning, Ms. Brookes had something to tell the class. "We've had some excellent ideas for this year's special community project, but I have chosen the winner!" she had said.

When she had explained what they were going to do, some of Kitty's classmates had seemed a little nervous about visiting the house on the hill, and even frightened, until Kitty had told them all about Mrs. Thornton and how kind she really was. She couldn't wait for them all to meet her themselves.

As she reached the top of the hill, Kitty saw Mrs. Thornton waiting on the steps of her house, and waved. "Hi, Mrs. Thornton! We're here!" she called.

Mrs. Thornton beamed at Kitty. "This is just wonderful!" she said. "I'm so thrilled to see you all. I've baked lots of cookies and cupcakes to keep your strength up, and there's homemade lemonade too."

"Wow, she *is* nice!" Jenny whispered to Kitty, smiling.

Ms. Brookes split the class into groups: one to sweep leaves into piles, one to pull up weeds, and one to plant seeds. Everyone got to work, and Mrs. Thornton walked around carefully to hand out treats and talk to each person.

As Kitty and Jenny scattered their seeds, Kitty felt something soft and warm brush against her ankle.

"Shadow!" she said, bending down to stroke him. Turning quickly to make sure Jenny wouldn't be able to hear her, she leaned a bit closer and whispered, "It's lovely to come back and see you again. And you might see me later on—but I'll be on four paws instead of two feet!" She grinned as

Shadow gave an eager meow and purred. Although she couldn't understand what Shadow was saying, she could tell he was happy.

That night, Kitty returned to Mrs. Thornton's house—just as she'd promised Shadow—but this time she padded lightly up the hill in her cat form, with her tail waving behind her. Grandma ran next to her, and some of her cat friends followed: Misty, Tiger, Ruby, and Bella. Everyone was curious to see what Kitty and her class had done!

"Kitty, it looks wonderful!" purred Grandma as the house and yard came into view. In the moonlight, the neat

rows of flowers, plants, and herbs were clear, and the grass on the lawn was neatly trimmed.

"It looks so different. Not spooky at all!" added Misty.

"My human loves it, and so do I!" piped up a happy voice nearby.

The cats turned to see Shadow— who was sitting *outside* the garden fence! "Shadow, you're not staying inside your house or your yard anymore!" meowed Kitty.

Shadow padded forward to bump foreheads with Kitty and all the other cats. "That's right! I don't need to be worried about my human. She made lots of new friends today. And I've made lots of new friends too!" he added, purring shyly.

Grandma gave Kitty a nudge with her nose. "Well done, Kitty!" she whispered. "I'm so proud of you. Being brave and kind and friendly are all very important parts of being a Guardian, and I can see from how well you've helped Shadow that you're good at all three of those things!"

Kitty purred happily. "Thank you, Grandma," she whispered back. "I love all the things I'm learning about being the Guardian. And most of all? I love, love, *love* being a cat!"

MEET

Kitty

Kitty is a little girl who can magically turn into a cat! She is the Guardian of the Cat Council.

Tiger

Tiger is a big, brave tabby tomcat. He is leader of the Cat Council.

Suki

Suki is Kitty's grandmother. She can magically turn into a cat too!

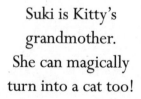

THE CATS

Shadow

Shadow can be
very shy with new
cats. He is amazing
at climbing trees.

Pinky is a very rare
breed of cat without
any hair at all! She is
wise and friendly.

Pinky

Bella

Bella is an excitable
kitten! Her coat is
made up of many
different colors.

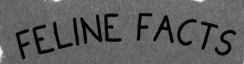

FELINE FACTS

Here are some
fun facts about our
purrrfect animal friends
that you might like
to know…

Cats close their
eyes when they
are **happy**.

Cats can't taste
sweet things.

3.

Every cat's nose is as unique as a **fingerprint**.

4.

Cats **always** land on their feet.

5.

Cats can make over **one hundred** different sounds.

Kitty's Magic

Ruby the Runaway Kitten

Chapter 1

"Yes! I'm nearly at the end of level three!" said Kitty Kimura excitedly, pressing the buttons on her game controller. "I just have to jump over this puddle, tiptoe past the dog kennel, and I'm almost home."

"Go on, Kitty!" cried her best friend, Jenny. "I love this part of the game."

"Me too," added their friend Evie. "You're so good at it, Kitty!"

It was spring break, and Kitty and Jenny had been invited to Evie's house for the afternoon. They had made up a dance routine in the backyard, then tried out Evie's glittery felt-tips, all the while playing with Evie's gorgeous new kitten, Ruby. Ruby was only a couple of months old, and she was a very special breed of cat called a Bengal. This meant that her fur was almost golden, with dark spots that made her look like a tiny, adorable leopard. Now the girls were playing an exciting new game called Catventure on Evie's games console, taking turns playing the game and fussing over the kitten.

"How many of your nine lives have you used up, Kitty?" joked Evie.

Kitty giggled as she finished the level and handed her controller over to Jenny. She was eager to get back to playing with Ruby. She bent down to tickle Ruby's soft tummy, grinning as the kitten rolled around happily on the carpet. Evie grabbed the fishing-rod cat toy that they'd been playing with and dangled it over Ruby, who swatted playfully at the little stuffed fish on the end of the line.

But Evie frowned as a high-pitched wail broke out, which they could easily hear even over the noise of the computer game. "Dad!" she yelled. "He's crying again!"

Evie's baby brother, Joe, was strapped

into his bouncy chair near the television. He was just three months old, with big brown eyes and lovely chubby cheeks. Kitty thought he was so sweet. He had been napping when the girls came in, but the music from their game must have woken him up, and now he was crying noisily.

"Come on then, young man!" said Evie's dad cheerfully as he breezed in, unbuckling the straps on the bouncy chair and gently picking Joe up. "Let's go wander around the backyard, shall we, so we don't disturb your big sister and her friends?"

As her dad stepped outside, Evie sighed. "Joe cried for hours last night too," she explained to Kitty and Jenny.

"Mom and Dad and I were all watching a movie together, but we kept having to pause it. In the end it got too late and I had to go to bed without watching the ending. Dad even said he'd make us some popcorn, but he didn't have time. Baby brothers are cute, but they can be so annoying!"

"Definitely!" agreed Jenny, grinning. "Although Barney's a lot of fun, now that he's a bit older."

Kitty smiled. She was an only child, but she'd always wanted a little brother or sister, so secretly she thought Evie was really lucky. Baby Joe *did* need lots of attention, though!

Ding-dong! The doorbell rang, and Kitty heard Evie's mom go answer it.

"Hello, Mrs. Kimura! Come on in. Kitty's just with the girls in the living room."

"Hi, Grandma!" called Kitty. She gave little Ruby one last tickle and then ran into the hall to give her grandmother a hug. Grandma lived with Kitty and her parents, so Kitty and Grandma were very close. Grandma was from Japan, and she had the same dark eyes and straight, shiny black hair as Kitty— though Grandma's bob had a streak of pure white running through it.

"Hello, my darling," said Grandma. "Have you had a nice afternoon? Mom and Dad are staying late at the shop tonight, so it's going to be just the two of us."

Kitty's parents owned a little shop on Willow Street, just around the corner from their house, which sold all sorts of special Japanese trinkets and objects. They often had to work late or take business trips to Japan, but Kitty didn't mind—it meant she could spend more time with her grandma.

Kitty said goodbye to Jenny and Evie and thanked Evie's mom for having her. She peeped out of the kitchen window and waved goodbye to Evie's dad, who was still strolling round the garden with baby Joe nestled in his arms, now fast asleep. Then she and Grandma began to walk home.

"It's such a lovely day. Let's go home through the park, shall we?" suggested Grandma. "I don't know about you, but I'd like to ride on the swings!"

The park was busy with children playing soccer, swinging on the swings, and feeding the ducks at the edge of the park's small pond. Grandma nodded toward a quiet shaded area underneath a row of oak trees nearby. Three cats

were playing in the grass, pouncing on each other and tumbling around. Kitty realized that one of them, a small silver tabby, was Jenny's cat, Misty.

Grandma winked at Kitty. "If you're careful, you can go and play with the cats for a little while before dinner," she whispered.

Kitty looked at Grandma's mysterious expression, then grinned. She understood exactly what Grandma meant. Kitty had a very special secret, and Grandma was the only other person in the world who knew it!

For her whole life, Kitty had loved cats, but she had always thought she was allergic to them. Her nose itched, twitched, and tickled whenever she was anywhere near a cat. Then one day, Grandma had given Kitty a gift: a pretty silver necklace with some strange words engraved on it. That night, Kitty had stayed over at Jenny's house, and she'd had a sneezing fit that she'd thought was because of Misty, Jenny's cat. But to her amazement, something magical had happened. Kitty had turned into a cat!

Grandma had explained to Kitty that her amazing ability had been passed down through the family for years and years. She said that the special necklace's words would help Kitty to change back and forth from human to cat whenever she wanted to. Kitty thought she was the luckiest girl in the world. And over time, she had been getting better at using her magical power. She loved padding around her town after dark in her cat form, when all her human friends were tucked up in bed. She especially loved making friends with the other cats she met, including her very best cat friend, Misty. But Kitty had to be very careful not to let any other humans find out about her special gift. If they did, Grandma had explained that the magic would be lost forever.

Kitty glanced around to make sure that no one in the park was watching. She stepped behind a bush and reached for her necklace. Kitty took a deep breath. Then, very quietly, she muttered the mysterious words on the pendant.

"Human hands to kitten paws,
  Human fingers, kitten claws."

As a warm, tingling feeling swept through her fingers and toes, Kitty closed her eyes. Her legs, arms, and belly fizzed as though they were full of thousands of tiny lemonade bubbles. It felt like she was being tickled all over her body.

When the feeling stopped, Kitty opened her eyes. The first thing she noticed was that she could see every tiny detail on the bush in front of her: the pattern on the leaves, the droplets of rain from earlier that day, and even a row of ants scuttling along. She glanced down and instead of her hands she saw two small white, furry paws, with neat little claws, at the end of fuzzy black legs. Her silver necklace had been replaced by a pretty collar with a tiny picture of a girl engraved on it. Kitty was a cat!

Chapter 2

Kitty trotted out from behind the bush and ran to join the cats playing under the oak trees. She loved the feeling of the grass beneath her paws and the swish of her tail behind her. When Misty caught sight of Kitty, the little silver tabby let out a happy meow.

"Hi, Kitty! I was hoping you'd come out to play today!"

Kitty bumped heads gently with Misty to say hello. She knew the other cats too: a friendly, fluffy gray named Smoky, and an excited young tortoiseshell called Bella. They all purred a greeting, and another cat appeared by Kitty's side: a small black cat with a patch of pure white fur by one of her ears.

"Suki!" said Bella.

Kitty purred happily. "Hi, Grandma," she meowed, bumping heads with the small black cat. Kitty wasn't the only human with the special ability to turn into a cat—her grandma could do it too! Kitty still found it incredible— and, of course, it meant she had another amazing thing in common with her grandmother.

Kitty and her grandma joined in as the cats gathered under a nearby tree, eagerly eyeing the small birds collecting in its branches. They meowed in disappointment as the birds suddenly scattered, flying up into the sky—but they were soon distracted by a game of chase with a couple of butterflies that

were fluttering past. The cats ran after them happily, swatting at them as they danced through the air. Kitty still wasn't sure why chasing after things was so much fun as a cat, but she definitely enjoyed it as much as the others did!

"Oh, look, there's Coco!" meowed Bella breathlessly, nodding toward a cat which was a short distance away. "And who's that kitten with her? I've never seen her before."

Kitty watched as Coco padded over to them to say hello. Coco was an elegant British Shorthair, with thick blue-gray fur, gleaming golden eyes, and a beautiful velvet collar. Coco could sometimes be a little bit snooty, but most of the time she was friendly with the other cats in town. Today, though, Kitty sensed she was in a bad mood.

"Hi, Coco," Bella said. "Who are you with?"

"Oh, that's Ruby," Coco meowed grumpily, nodding at the kitten eagerly trotting along behind her. "My humans adopted her last week."

Kitty smiled over at Ruby. "I met little Ruby at your house today, Coco," Kitty replied. "I know your humans— Evie's one of my school friends, and I was playing at her house this afternoon!" That was another one of the nice things about Kitty's special gift: she often knew both the humans and the cats in one family. Evie and her parents were Coco's owners. When they'd heard that a kitten needed a new home, they'd decided she would be good company for Coco. Kitty thought that Coco didn't seem very happy about it all, though. She curled her tail around her body primly and sighed.

"Yes, I was playing in the yard next door, but I could hear you all making a fuss over Ruby," Coco said, sounding a bit annoyed.

Just then, Ruby caught up with them and gave a bright, cheerful meow. "Hello, big cats!"

The other cats meowed in greeting too.

"Hi, Ruby!" Kitty replied with a friendly meow. "Nice to see you again!

I'm Kitty. We met earlier at your
house."

The leopard-like kitten looked a bit
confused. "Were you hiding at the end
of the yard? That's where my friend
Coco goes sometimes, and I have to go
and find her!"

Coco flicked the tip of her tail and Kitty thought she saw her roll her eyes.

"No, I was one of the girls that was playing with you and your human, Evie! I have a special ability, you see—I can turn into a cat!"

Ruby ran around in a circle, her fur ruffling, and did a little bounce. "Wow! That's amazing! I've never heard of a human who could be a cat too!"

Kitty giggled and then noticed that Ruby's small paws were covered in mud.

"She's been playing in a dirty puddle," Coco told them, shuddering as Ruby trotted away, curious about a black beetle that was crawling past. Coco always took great care with her grooming, and she seemed irritated that two of the other cats were meowing to each other about the lovely pattern on the little kitten's coat, when Ruby didn't even care about how she looked.

"It must be nice to have a new young cat at home to play with," said Bella wistfully.

But Coco wrinkled her nose. "It's so annoying," she grumbled. "Ever since Ruby arrived, my humans have barely paid any attention to me. If they're not cooing over their new baby, they're playing with Ruby and taking pictures of her with their hand-screen things. They seem to think everything she does is funny and cute."

Just then, Ruby caught sight of the pond nearby. With an excited mew, she dashed over to it, pouncing playfully toward a duck that was snoozing in the sunshine at the water's edge. With a squawk of surprise, the duck flapped his wings and took off into the air, splashing water everywhere— including over Coco!

"Ugh! I hate getting wet!" snapped Coco, shaking the droplets of water out of her fur.

The other cats giggled as Ruby bounded around happily, enjoying all the new sights and smells of the park, but Kitty watched Coco bristle angrily.

I'd better keep an eye on Coco and Ruby, Kitty thought. *Coco can be a little bit mean*

when things don't go her way. This could lead to some trouble!

The following evening, Kitty was reading a book in the backyard when she caught sight of a symbol scratched into a tree trunk nearby: three small claw marks in the shape of a triangle. Kitty knew instantly what that symbol meant: one of the neighborhood cats wanted to call a meeting of the Cat Council. Local cats scratched that symbol into posts and trees whenever they needed to call a meeting, and Kitty knew that she needed to be there.

The Cat Council was a secret gathering of all the cats in town. Its job was to listen to any problems the cats had, and to try to help solve them. Tiger, a rather bossy but kind tomcat, was the leader of the Cat Council, but Kitty had a very special role too. She was the Guardian, which meant it was up to her to give advice to any cat in need. The other cats particularly liked to ask for Kitty's advice whenever they had a problem that had something to do with humans. Of course, Kitty understood the human world in a way all the ordinary cats couldn't! Grandma had been the Guardian before Kitty, and Kitty was very proud to have taken over, even though she still had things to learn.

A couple of hours later, Kitty was waiting impatiently for dinner to be over so that she could make up an excuse to go to bed early. When she was finally allowed to leave the table, Kitty helped Grandma clean up and whispered to her about the symbol she'd seen in the yard.

"We'd better both go there as soon as we can, Kitty!" replied Grandma.

After pretending to go to bed early, Kitty and Grandma transformed into their cat forms and slipped through the open kitchen window. Kitty loved padding through the town on a spring evening. The air was always full of interesting smells, and Kitty's cat nose was very sensitive. She could smell flowers and herbs from the yards and, of course, the scents of every single

cat in town. Each cat had a different scent, and Kitty was getting to know them all, one by one.

She followed Grandma up the street, leaped nimbly over a fence, ran along a wall, and finally made her way through an alleyway to the woods. The Cat

Council always met in the same clearing, and up ahead Kitty could see that a circle of cats had already started to gather. There were cats of every different kind in the Council, from tough old tomcats to elegant purebreds with pedigrees.

Kitty bumped heads with all her friends, including a quiet black cat named Shadow and a shy little kitten called Petal. She took her place in between Tiger and Grandma. When the last cats had arrived, Tiger started the meeting.

"Good evening, everyone! Settle down, please! Let's begin by saying the Meow Vow," he told them.

Together, all the cats in the circle recited the words that they said at the start of every Cat Council meeting:

"When you meow,
  We promise now,
  This solemn vow,
  To help somehow."

"Excellent!" said Tiger. "Now, which cat called this meeting? Please step forward and tell us how we can help."

To her surprise, Kitty saw Coco step primly onto a tree stump in the middle of the circle. Coco always attended the Cat Council meetings, but she had never called one herself before. Kitty glanced around to see where Ruby, the little kitten who now shared Coco's house, was sitting. There were a couple of other small cats around the circle, but Ruby wasn't one of them . . .

Suddenly, Kitty thought she could

guess what Coco was about to ask the Cat Council for help with. She just hoped she was wrong.

"*I* called this meeting, Tiger," Coco announced, swishing her fluffy tail. "I have something very important to discuss. It's about the kitten my humans have just adopted—Ruby."

"And is Ruby here today?" asked Tiger, glancing around.

Coco shook her head. "She's too little to know about the Cat Council, and I'm afraid I made sure not to tell her about the meeting," she explained.

"Oh. I hope nothing too serious has happened. Do tell us what the problem is," meowed Tiger, looking concerned.

Coco paused dramatically, looking around the circle. "I've decided that enough is enough," she declared. "It's just not fair, and I don't want that little fluff ball around any more. Ruby *has* to go!"

Chapter 3

All around the circle, the cats gasped.

Tiger shook his ginger head, looking very worried. "The Cat Council wants all cats to feel welcome in our town," he explained. "We would never want to force any cat to leave!"

There was a chorus of agreement from around the circle.

"I don't mind if Ruby stays in town,"

Coco told Tiger sulkily, "but I don't want her to live in my house any more."

"Why do you feel this way, Coco?" asked Grandma gently.

"Yes—Ruby's so pretty, and she seems so playful and fun!" added Misty.

Coco scowled. "That's just the problem!" she huffed. "She never sits still! She tries to play-fight with me all the time, and messes up my lovely fur. She treads muddy paw prints through the kitchen. She drinks my milk, and she's even started taking cat naps in my special place underneath the radiator! But worst of all, my humans think everything she does is adorable. They don't pay any attention to me any more, even though they've been my family for years and years. Now Ruby's come along and ruined everything! It's just not fair. I want another family to adopt Ruby instead, so that things can go back to the way they were before."

There were mutters of disapproval from around the circle. "Coco, you're just being selfish," meowed a Persian cat named Emerald.

Kitty agreed—but then she felt Grandma nudging her with a paw. "Kitty, as our Guardian, you must try to find a way to help Coco, as hard as that may be," she whispered.

Kitty hesitated. How could she help Coco? This felt like the hardest problem

she'd ever been faced with. She knew Grandma was right, though. She had to do her best. She took a step forward, and all the other cats hushed.

"Ah, Kitty! Perhaps our Guardian can think of an answer," said Tiger, sounding relieved.

"I hope so," answered Kitty. "Coco, I agree that Ruby seems like a bit of a handful at the moment, but don't you think that's just because she's so young? She's only a baby, really, and she's getting used to her new home. Over time, I think you might grow to like her. You might even find out that you have something in common."

"Kitty's right!" meowed Bella, and next to her, Misty nodded.

But Coco didn't look very impressed. "That advice is no help whatsoever," she told Kitty snootily. "I don't *want* to wait around for Ruby to grow up. I need things to change right now!"

Kitty didn't know what to say. Since she'd become the Guardian, she'd always been able to come up with a solution for every problem—until this one! "Er . . . I'll think of another way to help, I promise," she told the irritated cat.

"Hmm. I don't think so," huffed Coco, turning her back on Kitty, stepping down from the tree stump and slinking away.

"Maybe you have lots of human knowledge, Kitty, but you don't know enough about cats to help me out. This was a waste of time! I'm going home."

As Coco disappeared from the clearing, Kitty took a deep, shaky breath. The circle of cats began meowing and muttering anxiously, although Tiger tried to call for quiet. Grandma rubbed her head against Kitty's reassuringly, and Misty trotted up to her friend to give her a friendly head bump. "Don't listen to Coco, Kitty," Misty told her earnestly. "You're a great Guardian! Everyone says so."

"And you *will* find a way to help Coco," Grandma told Kitty. "I know you will!"

Kitty nodded. "I really hope so!" she meowed.

The question was—how?

Chapter 4

"Kitty, that was an awesome goal!" said Jenny as the girls walked out of soccer practice together the next day.

"Thanks!" replied Kitty, smiling. "You scored three! And you were great too, Evie," she added, catching sight of their friend walking over to join them.

Evie grinned at them. "I've been practicing my shots in the backyard," she explained. "Whenever I haven't been playing with Ruby, that is. She's just so sweet, I get distracted!"

Evie only talks about Ruby these days— never Coco, Kitty thought, as Evie chatted about her little kitten. Kitty felt a pang of sympathy for the grumpy pedigree cat.

"It's funny to think that you have two babies in your house at the moment," commented Jenny, smiling. "One cat baby and one human baby—Ruby and Joe!"

Kitty realized Jenny was right. Ruby was just like Joe: a new baby in the family! And maybe Evie and Coco were both feeling the same way: annoyed that the babies of the family were getting all the attention. Kitty decided to ask Evie if she was getting used to having Joe around now. As an only child, Kitty didn't know how it felt to have a new sibling, but Evie had been a big sister for three months. *She might have some tips or ideas that could help with Coco's problem*, Kitty thought.

"Jenny's right. You're really lucky, Evie!" she said. "Do you like being a big sister?"

Evie hesitated. "Sometimes," she admitted. "When Joe's being quiet and smiling, or he's giggling, then he's really cute. He's annoying when he cries, though—Mom and Dad just stop talking to me or listening to me and go straight to him. Once Mom was so

busy looking after Joe, she forgot to get my dinner out of the oven, and it burned! I think that's why they got Ruby for me," she added, "so that I wouldn't feel left out."

Kitty nodded, but nothing Evie had said had given her any ideas about how to help Coco.

All the way home, Kitty thought about Coco's problem. Finally, as she sat down for dinner with Grandma and her parents, she decided what to do. *I'll pay Coco a surprise visit tonight,* she thought. *Talking to Evie didn't help, but talking to Coco again might.*

That night, as soon as she heard her parents' bedroom door close, Kitty crept downstairs and into the moonlit yard. Very quietly, she whispered the words on her silver pendant and transformed into her cat form.

Kitty scrambled up onto the roof of her playhouse and from there leaped onto the top of the back fence. Using her tail, her whiskers, and her strong, sharp claws for balance, she ran nimbly along the fence, through her neighbors' yards, past the park, and then down the next street. Evie lived in a little cottage just past the post office.

Kitty darted into the backyard. Evie's toys were scattered all over the grass, and Kitty saw a clothesline full of tiny baby clothes swinging gently in the breeze. Now that she was here, she was a bit nervous. Coco hadn't exactly been friendly the last time Kitty had seen her. Still, she took a deep breath and was about to nudge the cat flap open with her head when she heard a curious meow behind her.

"Kitty? Is that you?"

Kitty whirled around, her fur standing on end in surprise. Coco was curled up on Evie's trampoline, her golden eyes gleaming in the darkness.

"You made me jump, Coco!" Kitty meowed. "What are you doing?"

Coco looked very sulky. "Trying to get some sleep," she answered. "I used to sleep on Evie's lovely, cozy bed before that stupid fluff ball arrived. Now Ruby sleeps there instead. I know you think

I'm just being selfish, but how would *you* like it if that happened to you?"

Kitty nodded. "It does sound difficult, Coco," she admitted. "I really want to find a way to help you. That's why I'm here!"

"Come inside," Coco told her, jumping down from the trampoline and trotting daintily over to the cat flap. "Then you'll see for yourself."

Kitty followed Coco through the cat flap and into the darkened kitchen. This was the first time she'd ever been in Evie's house in her cat form, and it felt really strange! Kitty stared around, her sharp cat eyes and ears picking up details she'd never noticed before, like the pattern of tiny dots on the tablecloth

and the whispery rustle of the plants on
the window sill.

"Look!" said Coco, swishing her
thick furry tail.

Kitty looked at where Coco's tail was
pointing and saw an elegant china bowl
on the kitchen floor, with *Coco* written

on the side in swirly letters. Chunks of cat food were splattered all around it. "That's *my* special bowl, and Ruby thinks she can just help herself without asking," Coco explained. "She makes such a mess!"

"She *is* just a kitten," Kitty replied hesitantly. "I bet all kittens are messy eaters, Coco."

Coco snorted. "Not me! I was always a very delicate eater," she told Kitty. "And look up there, on the fridge."

Kitty glanced up and saw a series of photographs stuck to the fridge with magnets. Most of them were of Evie and Joe, but there were also three pictures of Ruby. In one of them, she was cuddled sweetly on Evie's lap. In the second, she was reaching a tiny paw up to touch a butterfly. In the third, she was chasing after a bouncy ball, with Evie giggling in the background. Kitty quickly scanned the rest of the pictures, but none were of Coco.

"See? She's taken over everything," Coco said angrily.

Kitty felt awful. She really could understand why Coco was so upset about Ruby. But she still couldn't see a way to help. "Where is Ruby now, Coco? Maybe we could try talking to her about this," she suggested.

"Probably curled up on Evie's bed— like I said, she sleeps there now," said Coco, padding into the hallway and up the stairs.

Kitty trotted after Coco, who nudged open the door to Evie's bedroom with her paw and nose. Peering inside, Kitty saw Evie snuggled under her star-patterned duvet—and curled up at the end of the bed was a tiny, fluffy heap.

"See? That's where *I* used to sleep," muttered Coco.

The spotted golden heap stirred, and Ruby lifted her head and blinked sleepily. "Coco?" she meowed. "And . . . Kitty! Have you come to play?" Suddenly, the little kitten was wide awake!

Kitty couldn't help giggling as Ruby sprang down from the bed excitedly and ran forward to bump heads with her. Coco narrowed her eyes, annoyed.

"What should we do? Should we play a game? We have lots of toys, don't we, Coco?" said Ruby eagerly.

"They're my toys, actually," Coco replied coldly. "And you're too little to play with us anyway, Ruby."

The kitten looked hurt, and Kitty felt sorry for Ruby. But before she could say anything, there was a wail from down the corridor. Kitty felt her ears prick up and saw Coco's and Ruby's do the same. Baby Joe had woken up, and he was crying—very noisily!

"Quick!" whispered Kitty urgently. "If Evie wakes up, she'll see me in her bedroom, and I'm not supposed to be here! I need to get downstairs, fast."

"Let's go!" agreed Coco, darting out of the bedroom and into the corridor. Kitty followed her, and she heard the tiny pad of Ruby's paws behind her as well.

"What an unhappy sound that is!" Kitty heard Evie's dad saying gently. "Come on now, shhh."

"Dad?"

Kitty froze at the top of the staircase, and her ears pricked up again as she heard Evie call out sleepily.

"Oh dear," said Dad, "it sounds like your big sister's awake now too."

"I'm just going downstairs to get a drink," said Evie.

"Okay, love. Back to bed straight after that," Evie's dad called back.

Kitty and the others darted down the stairs, but she heard the thump of Evie's footsteps coming soon after. There wasn't time to run for the cat flap. Evie would be in the kitchen at any moment!

Chapter 5

Kitty turned to Coco. "Where should I hide? I can't let Evie see me!" she whispered anxiously.

"Over there, behind the recycling bin," suggested Coco. "Quickly!"

Kitty dashed into the kitchen and crouched behind the big green recycling bin. She tucked her white-tipped tail in and flattened her ears so that nothing was poking out. Just as she did, the kitchen door opened wider and the light came on. Kitty heard Evie step into the kitchen.

"Ruby! What are you doing down here? You were cuddled up on my bed when I went to sleep," Evie cooed down at the little kitten.

Kitty peered carefully around the recycling bin and saw her friend bend down and gently scoop Ruby up.

Evie stroked the fur between the kitten's ears, while Ruby purred happily. "Maybe you're hungry," Evie suggested. "How about a little snack?"

Kitty watched as Coco rubbed against Evie's ankles, meowing hopefully. To her surprise, Evie didn't even glance

down at Coco. She was paying too much attention to Ruby to even notice her older cat. *Evie's not behaving very fairly*, Kitty thought to herself. *Poor Coco.*

Evie put Ruby down and rummaged in a cupboard. She pulled out a box and scattered a handful of kitten treats in a little saucer, placing it on the floor next to Ruby. As Ruby dug in happily, Evie went over to the sink and ran herself a glass of water. She called, "Night night, Ruby!" then headed back upstairs, switching the light off as she went.

Kitty waited for a moment or two while her cat eyes adjusted to the dark again. When she was sure the coast was clear, she stepped out from her hiding place. She had decided she would talk to Evie at school tomorrow and try to put in a good word for Coco. If Evie gave *both* cats lots of love and attention, Coco wouldn't feel so left out.

But as she was about to explain her plan, Coco let out a nasty growl.

"It's not fair!" the gray cat snapped,

reaching out a fluffy paw and knocking Ruby's dish of kitten treats over. As the food scattered over the floor, she turned to the tiny kitten so that they were whisker to whisker. Angrily she hissed, "I wish you'd just go away, Ruby. And never come back!" And with that, she stormed across the kitchen and out of the cat flap.

Ruby was wide-eyed as the cat-flap door swung closed again. Kitty understood why Ruby was a bit taken aback. Coco could be quite scary when she was angry.

"Why is Coco being so mean?" Ruby asked, sounding confused. "What did I do?"

"Oh dear. Don't worry, Ruby. Coco's just a bit upset right now. Everything will be okay," she reassured the kitten. "I'm going to find a way for you and Coco to get along, I promise!"

Kitty walked into school the next morning feeling very determined. She wasn't sure how to help Ruby and Coco in her cat form, but at least there was one thing she could do as a human. *I'm going to find Evie as soon as I arrive,* she told herself. *I'm going to talk to her about Coco, and tell her that she needs to pay attention to* both *cats!*

But when Kitty spotted Evie in the playground, she immediately knew that something was wrong. Evie's face was pink and blotchy, as if she had been crying, and Jenny had a comforting arm around their friend.

"What happened, Evie?" Kitty asked, rushing over to her. "Is everything okay?"

"It's my kitten, Ruby!" Evie said with a sniff, her eyes filling with tears. "She's gone missing!"

Chapter 6

"What? What do you mean, gone missing?" asked Kitty, shocked.

"Ruby wasn't in the house or the yard this morning," Evie sobbed. "She sometimes goes exploring, but she's always back at breakfast time. She's never missed it before, not once. Mom and Dad helped me look for her before school, but we couldn't find her anywhere. I'm so worried something awful has happened to her!"

"I'm sure she'll be okay, Evie," said Kitty, hugging her friend. "I bet by the time school finishes today, she'll have turned up. And if she hasn't, we'll help you look for her."

Poor Evie was upset and anxious all day and couldn't concentrate on her schoolwork. When it was time to go home, Kitty's class ran outside to the school gates. Evie's dad was there to pick Evie up, and Kitty could see from the worried look on his face that Ruby hadn't been found yet.

Grandma was picking up Kitty and Jenny today, and Kitty quickly explained what had happened.

"We'll have a good look on our way home, girls," agreed Grandma, looking very serious. "That poor little kitten . . ."

Kitty, Jenny, and Grandma walked home very slowly. Grandma glanced over hedges, and Kitty paused to check underneath every parked car they passed. They all called Ruby's name loudly, and Jenny even peeped inside one or two garbage cans, just in case Ruby had somehow fallen inside. But by the time they reached their street, there had been no sign of her.

Suddenly, Kitty had an idea. The other *cats* in town might be able to help search for Ruby! They were much more likely to know places a cat might hide. Kitty waited until Jenny had stepped inside her house and closed the front

door. She quickly glanced around to make sure that no one else was nearby except Grandma. "I think we'd better change into our cat forms, Grandma. I have to call a Cat Council meeting right away!"

Grandma nodded. "I think you're right, Kitty," she said, looking worried. Together, they hid behind a tall rosebush in the yard and, a few moments later, trotted out on their paws. But just as Kitty was about to scratch the special triangular symbol into a nearby telephone post, she saw Misty dart out of her front yard, her big blue eyes wide.

"Oh, Kitty, Suki, thank goodness," the silver tabby panted. "An emergency Cat Council meeting has just been called!"

Kitty and her grandma exchanged glances. Who could have called the meeting already?

Together, Kitty, Misty, and Grandma raced toward the woods, their tails streaking out behind them. As they padded into the clearing, Kitty was surprised to see more cats gathered there than she had ever seen before. It seemed like not only were all the cats from town there, but all the cats from the neighboring towns too!

"When I found out that a little kitten had gone missing, I just had to come along and help," Kitty heard Pinky, an unusual cat with no fur, explain.

"So did I!" agreed Sooty, a fluffy white cat with patches of black fur. "I hope we find her. The poor little thing must be so frightened."

"I bet her humans are worried sick!" added Shadow, the older, sleek black cat who Kitty had helped not too long ago.

Kitty ran over to sit beside Misty and Tiger. "Who called the meeting?" she asked breathlessly, still puzzled. *Who else knew that Ruby was missing?*

"Yes, who called this emergency meeting?" asked Tiger, addressing the whole group. "Please step forward."

Kitty gasped as *Coco* padded into the circle! Instead of acting sulky and cross, the elegant cat looked worried and frightened. Her whiskers drooped and her fur, usually so groomed and tidy, was sticking up messily.

"*I* called the meeting," she announced, her voice shaky. "I live with Ruby, the little kitten who's gone missing. I . . . I think it was all my fault!"

"Oh dear. Tell us what happened, Coco," Tiger encouraged her kindly.

"I was so nasty to her," Coco admitted. "I told her to go away. Then, by this morning, she had disappeared! I think she ran off because of what I said. I didn't really mean it, though. I just wish she'd come home safe and sound!"

"We'll find her, Coco," Kitty said.

"I should have listened to your advice, Kitty!" meowed Coco miserably. "I should have tried to get along with Ruby, instead of only thinking of myself. I feel terrible. I've been looking for her everywhere—in the yard, in our garage, even in the horrid cobwebby shed. That's why my fur's such a mess!"

"She can't have gone very far," Kitty reassured her. "I think we should all split up. That way, we'll be able to search more places. If we all get into teams of two, hopefully we'll find Ruby in no time."

"Good idea, Kitty!" agreed Tiger. "Let's see. Misty and Bruno, you take the playground. Petal and Emerald, you look around the park. Smoky and Shadow, check the alleyways . . ."

Tiger gave all the cats a different area to search. Kitty decided to go with Coco.

"Why don't we go back to your street, Coco?" Kitty suggested. "I'm sure Ruby won't have gone very far. Perhaps she's somewhere close to home."

"Check all the yards and under all the cars," Tiger called to the cats as they headed off. "Remember to look in playhouses and underneath trampolines too!"

"Come on, Coco!" said Kitty. "Let's go!"

The two cats raced back to Coco's street. As they ran toward Coco's house, Kitty saw Evie's dad sticking up a flyer to a lamp-post. It showed a picture of Ruby, with the word *LOST* scribbled above it in Evie's handwriting, and a phone number below. Evie's dad was holding a thick stack of the flyers, and Kitty guessed he was planning to stick them up all over town.

"Where shall we look first, Coco?"

Kitty asked, as Evie's dad walked further away down the street. "Any ideas? Where do you think Ruby might hide?"

Coco shook her head anxiously. "I don't know," she admitted. "I don't even know what Ruby likes, or where her favorite places are."

"Well, where would *you* go?" asked Kitty. "Imagine you're feeling sad, or grumpy, or you just want to be by yourself."

Coco paused, thinking hard. Then she looked at Kitty, her golden eyes wide. "That's it! I've thought of somewhere!" she said excitedly. "Thank you, Kitty! How could I not have thought of this before now? Follow me!"

Chapter 7

"Wait, Coco! Why are we going back inside your house?" said Kitty, puzzled as she followed Coco.

"That's just it! I think that's where Ruby might be," explained Coco.

Eagerly she leaped through the cat flap and ran up the stairs. Kitty followed, wondering if Coco was heading toward Evie's bedroom—but she was surprised to see Coco dart into baby Joe's room instead. Kitty trotted after her on her quick paws, feeling even more confused.

"You think Ruby's in here?" she asked Coco.

Next to Joe's empty cot was a comfy-looking rocking chair with a blanket spread over it. Next to that was a chest of drawers, painted white with a pattern of little bunnies. A wooden toy box was sitting on top of the chest of drawers. It was packed with stuffed animals, their fluffy ears poking out. But there was no sign of the little kitten.

Coco nodded at the toy box. "There!" she told Kitty. "Sometimes, when I'm feeling really bad, I go and sit in that

toy box. It's cozy and warm and quiet in there. Ruby might have seen me do it before and decided to hide there herself!"

Coco sprang onto the rocking chair, making it rock backward and forward. Taking a second to get her balance, she then jumped up onto the chest of drawers. Kitty did the same, landing with a gentle thud beside the gray cat. She peered inside the toy box with Coco, and they used their paws to push the teddy bears and soft toys aside. Suddenly there was a tiny squeak of surprise from inside the box, and something moved.

"I was right!" meowed Coco happily.

"Ruby!" cried Kitty.

A tiny spotted head slowly peeped

out from among the toys, and a pair of big eyes blinked nervously.

When Ruby saw Coco, she gave a yelp of worry and scrabbled to jump out of the box, as if she was about to run away again. Kitty gasped as the toy box wobbled with the sudden movement. "Ruby, don't move! The toy box

is right on the edge of the chest of drawers. If you jump out, I think it might topple off!" she warned.

"I'm sorry I was so mean to you, Ruby!" meowed Coco. "Please don't run off again. I promise I'm going to be nicer to you from now on."

But the little kitten was still upset and wasn't listening. With a meow, she leaped from the toy box down to the carpet. As she did, the whole box wobbled forward and tumbled down after her, with toys and teddy bears spilling out everywhere! The box landed upside down—with Ruby trapped underneath it!

"Ruby!" meowed Coco anxiously, jumping down quickly from the chest of drawers and pushing at the box with her paws. "Kitty, help! It's too heavy to move by myself."

Kitty jumped down too, but even when both cats tried nudging the box together, it didn't move. "Ruby, are you okay under there?" Kitty meowed to her worriedly.

"I think so," Ruby squeaked, her voice sounding muffled from under the box. "I'm not hurt. But it's very dark in here. I want to get out!"

Kitty's mind was racing. As a cat, she couldn't help Ruby, but if she turned back into her human form, she'd be able to lift the box easily! It would be very risky, though. If Evie or one of her parents found her there, her magical secret would be lost forever . . .

But Kitty didn't have time to make her mind up—there were footsteps in the corridor outside, and Evie's voice called, "Mom, is that you? I just heard a funny noise in Joe's room."

Kitty had to hide again! Quickly, she

squeezed underneath Joe's cot. Peeping out from underneath, she saw a pair of spotty yellow socks appear in the doorway.

"Coco!" Evie said, sounding very surprised. "What are you doing in here? Oh, you naughty cat! You've knocked over the toy box!"

No, she's not being naughty! Look underneath it! thought Kitty, silently pleading with Evie. *Look underneath the box!*

Coco was trying her best to show Evie what had happened. Meowing loudly, she patted the box with her paws and nudged it with her head.

"What are you doing, Coco? I don't have time to play with you. I've got to find Ruby," scolded Evie.

Hearing her name, Ruby let out a few squeaky little meows from underneath the box. Kitty held her breath.

"Ruby!" Evie cried. Kneeling quickly, she lifted the box. Ruby scampered out and pounced toward Evie's legs, rubbing against them and meowing excitedly. "You were here all along!" Evie said. "And it was Coco who found you. Clever, clever Coco!"

She bent down and picked up Coco, giving her a long cuddle. Coco purred happily, rubbing the top of her head against Evie's chin. Hidden under the cot, Kitty had to try very hard not to start purring herself, in case Evie heard the noise.

Ruby's been found safe and sound, and Evie knows that it's all because of Coco, she thought, watching Evie plant kisses all over Coco's head. *Maybe now she'll pay Coco more attention, and Coco and Ruby will get along better!*

"Kitty! Jenny! Guess what?" Evie called, running into the playground the next morning. "Ruby's okay!"

"Hooray!" cried Jenny. "Where was she?"

"She didn't run away. She was in our house all along!" explained Evie, laughing. "She'd been hiding in Joe's toy box. Mom and Dad couldn't believe it. We didn't even find her ourselves—it was Coco!"

"Wow! What a clever cat," said Kitty, with a secret smile to herself. "You must be really happy, Evie."

"Yes. I'm so relieved!" Evie agreed. "We've been totally spoiling *both* cats ever since we found little Ruby. Mom bought some special fancy cat food as a treat, and a new collar for each of them. Dad even said that both of them could sleep on my bed. I wasn't sure they would do it, because they'd never slept there together before, but they curled up in a furry ball side by side, purring! It was *so* cute!"

"You're so lucky, Evie," Jenny said as the three girls walked into their classroom, "having *two* gorgeous cats to play with!"

"I know! *And* a baby brother," said Evie happily. "When Ruby ran away, it made me realize how sad I'd be if anything bad happened to Joe. He's only little, just like her—I should be helping to look after him, not getting annoyed by him!"

Kitty grinned. It looked like helping Coco and Ruby had solved Evie's problem too!

That night, Kitty changed into her cat form once her parents had gone to bed. She leaped off her window, landing sure and steady on her four paws, and made her way straight over to Evie's street, hoping to find Coco and Ruby. She came across both cats playing in their backyard together.

"Hi, Kitty!" meowed Ruby cheerfully. "Coco's teaching me how to call a Cat Council meeting, in case I ever have to do it myself."

"That's great, Ruby," Kitty told the little kitten. "It must be lovely having an older cat like Coco to learn things from."

"Thank you, Kitty. You really helped me to see that I shouldn't just think about myself. I wasn't very nice to Ruby at first," Coco admitted sheepishly. "But I'm going to look after her from now on."

"It's so much fun doing things together!" Ruby purred, looking happily at Coco. "Guess what, Kitty? We've even tried cuddling up under the radiator together, and we both fit!"

"In fact, it's even cozier with two!" added Coco, chuckling.

Kitty giggled, delighted to see her friends getting along so well. She was happy too because, as Guardian, she had been able to help them out. Even

though this had been her trickiest challenge yet, she was already looking forward to her next cat adventure!

MEET

Kitty

Kitty is a little girl who can magically turn into a cat! She is the Guardian of the Cat Council.

Tiger

Tiger is a big, brave tabby tomcat. He is leader of the Cat Council.

Suki

Suki is Kitty's grandmother. She can magically turn into a cat too!

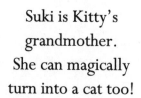

THE CATS

Ruby

Ruby is a kitten who always wants to play. Ruby is a Bengal kitten— which means she looks like a tiny leopard!

Coco is a very glamorous cat. She just loves to be the center of attention.

Coco

Smoky

Smoky is a plump, friendly female cat. Her fur is very fluffy and all her paws are white.

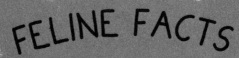

FELINE FACTS

Here are some
fun facts about our
purrrfect animal friends
that you might like
to know...

Cats hide when
they are **jealous**.

Cats can't see directly
below their **noses**.

3.

A cat can jump up
to **seven times**
its height!

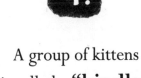

4.

A group of kittens
is called a **"kindle"**
and a group of cats is
called a **"clowder."**

5.

Cats can be **right-** or
left-pawed, the same
way people are right-
or left-handed!

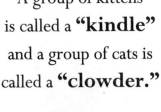

Join Kitty on her next adventure!

Kitty is going to her cousin's farm for the weekend!
There are lots of animals to meet, including Daisy,
an adorable black and white puppy, and Star, the old
farmhouse cat. Star's job is to chase mice away from
the strawberry harvest but it's become hard now that
he's older. Daisy wants to help, but
cats and dogs can't be friends . . .
can they?

Ella Moonheart grew up telling fun and exciting stories to anyone who would listen. Now that she's an author, she's thrilled to be able to tell stories to so many more children with her Kitty's Magic books. Ella loves animals, but cats most of all! She wishes she could turn into one just like Kitty, but she's happy to just play with her pet cat, Nibbles—when she's not writing her books, of course!

Magic Animal Rescue

BY E. D. BAKER

When magical creatures need help,
it's Maggie to the rescue!

Unicorn Princesses

BY EMILY BLISS

Welcome to an enchanted land ruled by unicorn princesses!

COMING SOON!

Don't miss Pippa's journey to find the golden horseshoes and save Chevalia!